A Beginners guide to Scandal

ALIVIA FLEUR

SPENCER & CO
PUBLISHING

A catalogue record for this work is available from the National Library of Australia.

Cover design by Evelyne Labelle at Carpe Librum Book Design www.carpe librumbookdesign.com

A BEGINNER'S GUIDE TO SCANDAL © 2023 by Alivia Fleur

For anyone who has held the hand of someone already gone.

Welcome to Honeysuckle Street

In a quiet corner of London, on the north side of the river, is a little street called Honeysuckle Street.

Don't bother looking for it now—you won't find it on any map. But once, before progress was the catchword of the day, Honeysuckle Street cut a treelined path between two main thoroughfares. The street itself could comfortably accommodate two carriages passing by one another. The residents spent their days in each other's company, or spotted one another on walks, or attended balls and gatherings together. A few errant children played games, and the odd elderly neighbour watched from behind twitching curtains, muttering about *young people these days*.

An enterprising developer had purchased the entire row on the north side of the street, cleared it and erected in its place five terrace townhouses. Five stories high, modelled on the Belgrave style and as similar on the outside as they were on the inside, which is to say, apart from the inhabitants, they were identical.

Five villas, each four or five stories high lined the opposite side of the street, mostly built at some stage during the reigns of the past kings named George.

And king of it all was a grey cat with a white-tipped tail named Spencer.

Spencer lived at number 6, the house in the middle of the street on the south side. It was rumoured that the old lady who occupied the house had been a lover of the Russian Tsar. Others said she had made and lost several fortunes in the American West. Others said that she had scrimped every penny she earned as a washerwoman and made a sensible investment during the last financial downturn. No one knew for sure. She didn't receive callers. She didn't make house calls.

She passed her time in the company of her beloved cats. At the end of each day, she stood on the porch and called them in. 'Mittens! Georgiana! Jimmy! Spencer! And no matter if they were curled up in the last ray of sun, or stalking along a limb, the little cats would run at the sound of her voice.

All except Spencer.

When he didn't return home, the old lady would wander the streets, calling and calling, 'Spencer! Spencer! Time for tea!' Later, when her hearing faded, she took to banging a pot with a spoon. When it suited him, Spencer would emerge, saunter his way to the house in the middle of the street, where the old lady would scald him but later, when sat by the fire, Spencer was still allowed to curl up and sleep on her lap.

When the old lady died, and unable to locate an heir, the authorities boarded up the old house. The furniture was pilfered. And after applying at kitchen doors, the kittens found new homes.

All except Spencer.

Spencer continued to patrol his street, hunting mice and chasing away noisier, bossier toms who might encroach on his territory. In return, the residents of Honeysuckle Street would find a scrap for him. Miss Delaney's cook left him the joint from the roast on Sunday. Miss Hartright put out a saucer of cream each night after her aunt had turned in. Mr Babbage put out a slice of cold ham, and not to be outdone, Mr Hempel left out two. The Caplin care-taker snuck him a biscuit, and in the evening, Miss Abberton left the downstairs window ajar so that he could squeeze himself inside and curl up by the furnace, even though he always managed to get by cook and took the best chair in the parlour instead.

Each morning and evening, Spencer sat on the decaying porch of the house in the middle of the street, silently surveying his charges. He kept watch on their comings and goings, their petty feuds and their longing looks over fences. He knew them all, sometimes better than they knew themselves.

Welcome to Honeysuckle Street.

WHO LIVES ON HONEYSUCKLE STREET?

February 1875

Number 1

Phineas Babbage, Bank Clerk

Number 2

Odette Delaney, Soprano

Number 3

Lawrence and Wilhelmina Hempel, Hotel Magnates and their children:

Rosanna

Johannes

Elliot

Beatrice

Garnett (deceased)

Amadeus

Nova

Ottile

Thaddeus

Number 4

Albert Abberton, Trader and businessman

Iris Abberton, Albert's adopted daughter

Number 5

Mrs Crofts, President of the Society for the Promotion of Civic Morality and the Adherence to Proper Values

Number 6

Vacant block mostly inhabited by Spencer, King of Honeysuckle Street

Number 7

Petunia Hartright, choir leader

And her niece

Elise Hartright

Number 8

Hamish Dalton, heir to Earl Caplin

Number 9

Benton Hunter, Diplomat, currently abroad

Number 10

His Grace Arley West, Duke Osborne

Prologue

October 1863

Iris knew where Hamish would be. She waited until the sun set and the house was not yet still, but only murmuring, before she crept from her bed. She threw a coat over her nightgown, tugged on her slippers, eased the window open, and swung her legs out onto the oak branch. Moving with a familiar purpose, she shuffled along, over the fence, the way she had for as far back as she could remember over her eighteen years, then dropped to land on the overgrown lawn of the abandoned villa at Number 6, Honeysuckle Street.

The earlier frantic conversations and garbled shouts still rang in her ears. The Dalton staff spoke high and frantic, conveying horrid news about an overturned phaeton. Hamish's father was abed and anguished, his mother had been injured badly and had died before arriving at the hospital, and Lewis, thrown hardest and furthest, was gone before the first passer-by had stumbled upon the twisted wreck. The horse, with two legs broken, had been the final casualty.

Throughout the afternoon, the rumour mill ground out grist of half-truths. Some said the earl, who had never been patient, had pulled too hard on the reigns and the horse had taken offence. Others suggested a robber from the shadows had upset the normally calm mare. The truth, when it was declared by the coroner, was more mundane. Moving too fast because they were late, a wheel had hit a rut in the road and the conveyance had tipped, spilling Hamish's family onto the street like milk.

Far worse than the idle speculation were the comments thrown by some of the staff that called to see if the Dalton's second son, now heir, was with his old friend, as no one could find him at home. 'He's a lucky one,' the maid had said. 'He gets to be earl now.'

Iris slipped through the backdoor of Number 6, and once inside, she felt his presence even before she heard his small sob. Fingers trailing over the peeling wallpaper and flaking paint, she followed the noise down the old hallway, calling softly to make sure he heard her approach. She navigated the staircase without thought, as she knew the path to avoid creaks and gaps, even in the dark, until she reached the old servants' quarters and cellars buried beneath the house. There, in the old kitchen, huddled over the open belly of the oven with an old flint they used to spark kindling, sat Hamish. His coat—one of the ill-fitting cast-offs that had been his brothers—lay discarded on the grubby floor, confirmation that money wasn't quite as lush as his family pretended. Iris took the flint and struck it, sparks flying into the cavity until a few landed on the paper, and she leaned over and blew gently, coaxing them into life. In silence they fed the small blaze some twigs, then sticks, until finally flames cast dancing shadows over the walls. Thin whisps of smoke puffed into the room, frail tendrils smelling of warmth and wood, like a memory already out of reach.

'Iris. They say that... Lewis. And my mother. Is it true?' He looked to her in desperation, and she knew that he wouldn't believe the rumours until she confirmed them. She nodded, and his face crumpled and distorted with pain. She thought he might start crying again, but he didn't, only shrank into himself as if crushed by the truth. Iris held out her arms and he curled into her side, the two of them breathing sadness into the chilled air of the kitchen. He laid his cheek against her breast, and Iris rested her chin on his unruly curls that smelt like orange water.

When she replayed the memory in her mind later, she could never be quite sure who found whose lips in the darkness, only that one moment they had clung to each other with the knowledge that everything they knew had shifted, and in the next they were pressed together. But she did know that she had been the one to find his collar and unfasten the mother-of-pearl button, and she had moved his hand to her thigh and encouraged him to explore her nakedness beneath her nightgown.

They had moved in sync, as they had always done. Offering and receiving. Giving and taking. Hamish spread his coat and bunched his shirt into a pillow, and she untied her hair so that it splayed behind her as she lay back, naked and shivering. He kissed the dip at the base of her neck, and his hands warmed her as his body chased away the chills.

Lips locked and hands intertwined, they moved like making love was a dance. And when it was over, they remained curled against each other until the black of night turned grey, then violet, and they helped one another dress. No words or empty promises, as neither of them had any certainty to give.

Later that day, Iris pressed her hand to the window and watched as Hamish, now changed into a black suit, walked down the stairs of Number 8, climbed into a carriage, and rumbled away. Not once did he look back.

Chapter One

February 1875

Twelve years later

The old house had been demolished.

Hamish shouldn't have been surprised. The place had been an eyesore and a death-trap when he was young. A dilapidated relic even in his earliest memories, Number 6 Honeysuckle Street had likely been built before the Peninsular Wars. The front door had always been boarded and nailed shut, while the back door wouldn't close. On cold days, the wind pushed itself through cracks in the walls and broken panes of glass, sending the scraps of curtains flickering.

Hamish's grandfather, may he rest in peace, had constantly bellyached about the state of the hideous building. When sufficiently roused, he would stamp his cane against the rug in time with each bellowed syllable until Hamish's father promised to write to the authorities, again.

Yes, it was a blessing that the old ruin had been knocked down.

And yet Hamish, Lord Dalton, heir to Earl Caplin, felt bereft. Twelve years had passed since he had last been in London, and when he recalled his childhood visits, the old house always figured in his memory. It had been the backdrop to many epic battles and adventures as he and the other spare heirs of the street played while nannies and maids gossiped. From the clacking shutters to the missing third stair, or to the cellar kitchen where they would light small fires in the old stove and make tea in a scavenged pot, or the treasure trove of busted furniture they used to build castles, it had all remained solid in his thoughts. For how long had he imagined it unchanged when here it was rubble?

A shadow shifted, and from behind a pile of bricks and dirt, a grey tail with a white tip flicked.

'It can't be.'

Hamish picked his way between the uneven bricks and clumps of weeds until he stood a few feet from the pile of debris, then he squatted down. As he tugged off his glove and extended his hand, he gave a low whistle before gently calling, 'Remember me?'

The raggedy tom regarded Hamish with narrow green eyes. His white whiskers twitched, sniffing the air, before he pushed his nose against Hamish's outstretched fingers and smooched against his palm. He could have walked straight from a memory. Spencer, the cat owned by no one and everyone, was somehow still alive, and judging by the slight paunch to his belly, was still king of Honeysuckle Street. As Spencer nuzzled into his palm, Hamish curled his fingers to scratch beneath an ear and was rewarded with a rumbling purr.

'I would advise against that.'

Hamish didn't want to break his reacquaintance with an old friend, so he remained squatting as he turned towards the street seeking the source of the comment. In the strained light of a mid-morning fog, he saw only the silhouettes of two women in walking attire. He couldn't clearly see their faces, but that voice... it wasn't so much the tone, which was deeper than the light, girlish tenor from his memory, but the all-knowing boldness that rang with incredible familiarity.

'All is well,' he called before running his palm down Spencer's back, who arched into the stroke with an extra loud purr. 'We're old friends.'

'Friendship won't save your suit, I'm afraid,' she called back. 'He's moulting.'

As if scalded, Hamish pushed himself to standing and clapped his hands together furiously. How had he not noticed? Flecks of fur wafted in the air, floating languidly before attaching to his suit as if it were magnetised. His trousers, brand new, were now sprinkled with specks of white and grey. Blast it. He'd need to change now before he went to the club.

A light laugh carried, high and bright, with the same assuredness that had chased him through streets and over fences all through his childhood. Never once giving a jot for who he was or who she was. After all this time, was she still living on Honeysuckle Street?

Hamish brushed the last of the fur from his palms. 'Do you know what happened to the house that used to be here?'

But when he looked to the street, the lady and her companion were gone.

Chapter Two

The thump of the front door closing smothered Iris's exhalation of relief. The February morning had been the warmest this week, which hinted at the impending summer heat that would round out the end of the stifling London season. Iris unbuttoned her coat and unpinned her hat. She fidgeted with its ribbons, uncoiling the loops until they were almost pulled loose.

Lord La-di-dah had returned.

'Are you well, miss?' Gena Tanner, her father's housekeeper and, in the absence of a suitable female relative, Iris's unwilling chaperone on her morning walks, took the hat and quickly rearranged the ribbons back into their proper place. 'Would you like tea?'

'In the study. Please.' Iris slipped off her gloves and tucked them into her pocket.

Even without Spencer's purr of approval, Iris would have recognised him. Yes, his chest had filled out and his shoulders had broadened. The mop of wayward curls had been replaced by a scrupulously tamed head of black hair, and his clothes had been made to size, a change from his brother's ill-fitted cast-offs. But the lanky boy, the one she had teased and chased and clambered through the back lanes of London with, his shadow remained etched in his easy gait, was tucked into the dimples of his confident smile, and still echoed in the impulsiveness of a man who would clamber over rubble in a good suit to stroke a street cat.

A question intruded on her reverie, and Iris had to blink hard to clear the whisps of memory. It would do no good to ruminate. Memories had no place in this house.

'Pardon, Mason?' The butler, Mason Richards, stood waiting in the hallway.

'Mr Sanders has come to call. He insists on seeing your father.' He spoke in an exaggerated stage whisper.

'But he was just here yesterday.' Panic gripped Iris and squeezed the breath from her lungs. 'Where is Papa?' she asked, her voice low.

'In the courtyard, napping. I asked Mr Sanders to leave his card, but he insists it is important *business*.'

'We can manage this.' Iris pinched her skirt between her fingers, bunching the flannel into her fists before releasing and smoothing the soft wool out again. 'Is Mr Rogers in?'

'He's seeing to the horses,' Mason replied.

'Right. If Papa wakes, have Mr Rogers keep him outside. And in about ten minutes, could you please interrupt us with an urgent message about something I must attend to.' Iris took a steady breath, fixed a smile, and took a step towards the sitting room.

'Excuse me, miss,' Mason hissed down the hall. 'What's the message?'

'What message?'

'The urgent message. What is it?' Mason asked.

'There is no message. I just need you to pretend there is one, so that I can make my excuses and Mr Sanders must leave.'

'But I can't deliver an honest line if I don't understand the meaning behind it.'

'Heavens help me,' Iris muttered. Like most of the people in their employ, Mason had found his way to them via her father's dear friend Jonah Worthington, who had a habit of saving wretches from ruin. Mason had come to London with theatrical dreams, but like so many who arrived in the capital, had supplemented his sporadic paid roles with small jobs, and then had entered service, before one day finding he was more staff than star. Mason's dream of walking the boards of the West End had never left him, and the old desire reared its head at the most inopportune moments.

'It can be any message. A fire in the kitchen. A note from Miss Delaney.' Iris smoothed her hair. 'Improvise.'

Mason's head bobbed in comprehension before he scuttled down the hall, calling 'Gena? Have you seen Mr Rogers?'

Mason disappeared around a corner and down the stairs to the kitchens. Curse Jonah and his West End failures. Iris found her most polite smile—not too enthusiastic, but not too dour—and stepped into the sitting room.

Mr Sanders, dressed in a neat black suit and plain grey waistcoat, stood half bent over a bookcase, squinting over his spectacles as he examined a lower shelf. The most junior investor on her father's board reminded Iris of a parrot she had seen in India whose owner had claimed could read, but instead squawked taught phrases when bribed with peanuts. He spoke with purpose and exactitude, but he lacked vigour or imagination. In the bright flamboyance of her father's favourite room, Mr Sanders appeared almost a shadow amid the brighter reminiscences of their lives.

Iris cleared her throat. Mr Sanders did not move. 'Mr Sanders,' she called, louder. 'A business call two days in a row. How pleasant.'

He startled, like a mouse caught by a lantern, hesitating on which way to turn. 'Miss Abberton. I have the files your father requested.'

Iris edged closer to the table and looked down at the stack of manila folders stuffed with cream papers, all tied together with a canary yellow cord. The long, flowing script on the top file read *Invoices and Returns – March 1874*.

'I asked for January, not March,' Iris said. She checked the title on the file underneath. *February*. Iris looked up, annoyed, then caught the slight frown creasing Mr Sanders's forehead. 'That is, Papa asked for January. He wanted to compare the previous year's figures for post-Christmas.'

'Is your father joining us? I wanted to speak to him on a business matter.'

'Papa is indisposed. But I can pass on any message you may have. Has the shipment from Lisbon arrived? He was very clear all three boxes were reserved for Mr Selfridge, he wanted exclusive—'

Mr Sanders waved his hand. 'The Lisbon shipments have been unloaded. There was some trouble at the docks, but nothing to concern you. Is he not in? I would really prefer to speak with him directly.'

'As I said, he isn't available, but if you tell me the issue—'

Before Iris could press Mr Sanders on what *trouble at the docks* meant, Gena backed through the doorway singing in a slightly off-key. 'Tea and scones, fresh from the oven. Fancy a hot bite of heaven, Mr Sanders?'

'I beg your pardon,' he said, his mouth slightly agape.

'You mentioned trouble at the docks.' Iris swerved around Gena to move closer to Mr Sanders. 'You didn't call the constabulary, did you? What were their complaints?'

'Fancy a squeeze?' Gena called, holding up a slice of lemon.

Mr Sanders flushed cherry red. Iris took a step closer. 'Was anything damaged?'

In the hallway a door slammed, and, beneath the tinkering of plates and cups, Iris could just make out her father's mumble, followed by the deep Welsh tones of Mr Rogers. 'Sir, please come pat the horse some more. He only nibbles, never bites.'

'Is your father really not in?' Mr Sanders's voice went up an octave. 'I thought I heard him arrive, just now—'

Annoyance and frustration spread warm through Iris's body. 'Are you being evasive, Mr Sanders? Because if there is a problem, then Papa needs to know.' If he would just tell her the issue, she could check the records, contact the more prominent men amongst the workers, and make any necessary arrangements to avoid disaster.

'Do you take sweetening, Mr Sanders? Sugar or honey? I have a lovely honeypot,' Gena called.

'The horse. Sir, please come back—'

Mr Sanders appeared as if he were about to burst, his furtive gaze darting between Gena, Iris, and the door. Chest swollen and his hands bunched into fists by his side, he stammered something about broken crates, then burst, 'I am not discussing the annual meeting agenda with a woman!'

Mr Sanders's voice cut sharp, and the following silence sent a cold trickle through the air. It wound its way beneath Iris's cuffs, skirted along her arms, and settled with an icy grasp along her back. Gena let a sugar cube drop into the cup with a *plop*. Mr Sanders, chest heaving slightly, brushed the top of his hat. How had a year already passed? How had she not noticed? Iris searched for words, but nothing other than *shipments* came to mind. A heavy step echoed through the hallway before, arms flung wide, Mason stepped into the sitting room and, with his booming stage voice, announced, 'My lady. Miss Odette is on fire!'

Iris closed her eyes and rubbed at her temples.

Mr Sanders, his breath still catching in the silence, took a step closer. 'I will send over the files for January. I can see myself out.'

Iris closed her eyes and let her ears follow Mr Sanders's tread down the hall, heard the door squeak open to let in the bustle of the street before it closed again. No one moved for a stretched silence, until Gena set the tea she had been preparing on the table, the saucer clinking softly against the wood.

A slight mumble and scuffle came from the hallway, and Papa's voice bounced into the room. 'Iris? Where is Iris?'

'I'm here, Papa.' She turned towards the door and reached out a hand as her father appeared. 'Come, sit in your chair.'

The first thing Iris always took in about her father were his eyes—were they calm? Scared? In this moment, they were wide, like a child who had found something new and couldn't decide if the discovery was safe or dangerous. As he shuffled across the room, he paused by the table to look at the folders, frowning. Iris watched him hard, willing him to acknowledge the word *Abberton* stamped across the front. He ran a finger over his surname. If he would show some spark of recognition, if he would just *remember*, maybe, like last year, she could send him to the meeting with enough notes to fumble through. For a moment, his eyes narrowed, before they turned soft. He turned away and continued his steady shuffle towards her.

Today was not a good day.

'This man made me pat his horse.' Papa pointed back to Mr Rogers who stood at the edge of the arch, scrunching his cap in his fists.

'I kept him as long as I could, miss,' Mr Rogers explained, his tone apologetic.

'No harm done. Gena, would you light the fire?' Iris took her father's hand and patted the thin, papery skin gently before leading him to his favourite chair. He had not had his gloves on, and he carried the outside chill with him. She helped her father lower himself against the cushion, then she knelt beside him. 'And did you like patting the horse?'

He thought for a moment. 'He nibbled my fingers.'

'You taught him how to do that. That's Socrates. He's your horse. Do you remember?'

Papa's eyes met hers, his pupils darting back and forth as he searched her face. He gave a slow nod. 'Yes. Socrates. He won something, didn't he?'

'A race, at a country meet. You bought him on the spot.' She darted across the room and plucked a gold cup from amongst the trinkets that lined the sideboard. 'Here,' she said, pressing it into his hands. 'He won this.'

Iris tucked her skirt beneath her and sat on Papa's footstool. He traced the engraving on the plaque, then looked up at her. 'Look, Iris. I won a trophy.'

In the early days they had laughed at Papa's forgetfulness. But, over time, it became more than just misplacing his spectacles or losing track of dates. He forgot conversations as soon as they ended, couldn't remember why he had come into a room, or talked about long forgotten things like they had happened yesterday. When consulted, the doctor had suggested a course of bloodletting. When Iris refused to consider it, he then advised stocking up on laudanum and muttered that she may want to consider commitment to Bedlam.

Iris bit her bottom lip and blinked fast until the mist in her eyes cleared. She squeezed her father's hand, before releasing it with a pang as she pushed herself up. The folders from Mr Sanders would not tabulate themselves.

Behind her, Gena, Mason, and Mr Rogers all stood frozen, their eyes locked on her. 'Back to work,' she snapped, her voice carrying more ire than she meant. All three of them startled and jerked into action so fast they almost fell over one another, like the vaudeville troupe they could have been.

'Make sure he's warm,' Iris muttered to Gena as she slid the folders from the table, hoping her tone conveyed some hint of an apology. She didn't have time for more. She had work to do.

CHAPTER THREE

Hamish watched the man saunter down the stairs of Number 4, tugging his gloves on as he went, before pulling himself into his trap and flicking the reigns.

'All done, my lord.' His valet held out his black coat, now devoid of fur. Hamish slipped his arms into its cavities and shrugged it over his shoulders.

'Irving, do you know that man?'

'I have been here only a day longer than you,' Irving said, not bothering to hide the slight annoyance in his voice. Like everyone in the Dalton staff, Irving had been hired by Hamish's father and had no loyalty to him. He briefly flicked the curtain back before letting the fabric fall over the glass. 'That is Mr Sanders.'

'Mr Sanders.' Hamish's eyes narrowed on the man's retreating form as an unwanted ripple of envy licked his insides. 'Who is Mr Sanders?'

'He is on the board of Abberton and Co Trading. He often calls on Mr Abberton.'

'For a man who has been in town barely a day, you seem to know an awful lot,' Hamish said.

'It is my business to know the business of the street. To know who may walk by and who is in residence.' He brushed the top of Hamish's hat. 'Besides, cook is a terrible gossip.'

Hamish couldn't help but give a small laugh. 'What else does cook say?'

'About Mr Sanders?'

'About the Abbertons. Is Miss Abberton still...' He couldn't quite finish the sentence.

'Still?'

'Still, well... *Miss* Abberton?'

Irving clicked his tongue. 'If I may be pertinent, sir?'

'You may not, but as my father pays you and not me, you will be regardless.'

'Sleeping dogs are best left asleep.'

Hamish grabbed his hat. 'For heaven's sake, Irving, we were *friends*. I can't call on a married woman without her husband's permission, can I? I don't have a companion in this city that my father hasn't arranged for me. At least allow me one independent friendship.'

Hamish pulled back the curtain and looked across the empty expanse of the vacant block. Spencer, that shedding demon who had delayed him, picked his way through the overgrown grass to a tree by the fence. He launched himself midway up the trunk with an agile leap, before clawing his way to a branch that sat level with the second story windows and tapping at the glass. The window sash lifted, and Hamish caught a flash of fine hands and the hint of blue sleeve. The cat leapt into the square abyss, and the window closed. The same window that Hamish had rapped on. Perhaps not everything had changed.

Hamish buttoned his coat, smoothed his handkerchief, and tugged at his pocket watch chain to check it would hold fast against a pickpocket.

'Have the carriage sent round,' he said. 'I best make an appearance at his damned club.'

Alone in the carriage, Hamish leaned forward and watched the city go by with a mixture of trepidation and excitement. Like the shock of finding the house in the middle of Honeysuckle Street gone—but Spencer still lording it over the rubble—the city was wrapped in strands of familiarity, yet parts of it felt strange and new. The curve of the Thames and the gleaming white bricks of the Tower were both familiar, yet the rapid construction of townhouses and new business blocks had turned many of his old haunts into a *terra incognita*. He felt himself poised between two paths: One well known, and the other shrouded in mystery but streaked with the promise of adventure.

He had known this city. Not from the luxury of a carriage rolling high above the street, but from the perspective of four foot and thin. He had spent those days running through alleys, sneaking apples from carts on a dare, or buying penny-lick ice cream from vendors in the park—which always tasted sweeter because his father forbade it. And the entire time, he had carved paths through it all with the wild girl two doors over, the girl with no mother to scold her and draw her inside to embroider or read or mind her constitution like every other society girl he knew.

With her, his visits to London had been a series of exciting escapades, until that last season twelve years ago. When he'd left the year prior, he'd said goodbye to a flat-chested, dirt-flecked, freckle-speckled girl the same height as him and just as weedy. The following summer, he had returned the same—thin, gangly, and still wearing his brother's altered tweed suit with a coat that hung too loose across the shoulders. But *she* had changed.

Where she had once been straight and flat, she had curves. Her long hair no longer hung in uneven, tousled plaits, but was set and pinned into place by the new lady's maid her father had hired. She had debuted at some ball, his mother said with a nonchalant air, not at court, *of course*, but her father's success at his trade still provided her with invites to all but the most exclusive events. Bitter envy had bit at Hamish, still confined to days in the house and evenings in the nursery. His brother Lewis tortured him with casual remarks about how pretty she looked, who she had danced with, and how many times. Some evenings, Hamish crept from his bed to sit on the back stair where he could hear his father and his friends weighing the worth of the latest debutantes, his skin searing when they spoke of the little miss two doors over. No title, but with tremendous wealth. Accomplished at piano, but mediocre at singing. A pretty mouth, but could it be tamed?

Back then, he had bunched his hands into fists and let his nails dig into his palm, as he did now. His anger concentrated and shredded his reverie. He should have anticipated a nostalgia at returning to his old haunts, but he needed to get over them fast. Those days were the folly of childhood, and long gone. He had his instructions from his father, and more than that, he had his own plan.

The carriage pulled up outside the Reform Club, one of three specified clubs he was permitted to attend. His membership had already been arranged, and after depositing his coat, Hamish followed a man to a table by the window, in the corner, and with a view of the stairs. His father's table, likely. Not long after came a cup of black tea with a slice of lemon and a copy of *The Times*.

For a man with arms that struggled to work, Hamish's father certainly had reach.

Settling into the brown leather chair, its back a soft, smooth embrace, Hamish flicked the paper open, his eyes skating over the day's news. Around him, men gabbled worse than hens, going on about some uproar in the house that afternoon, but after the dense silence of Caplin House, the chatter felt companionable. The sun glowed warm through the window. Tobacco smoke laced the air.

Perhaps the path his father had set wouldn't be such a bad existence. Moving between the estate and London. The sittings in parliament. Some titled chit on his arm who would provide a new heir and spare to please the old goat. A mistress in a small apartment across town. Hamish stretched, his back cracking, as if settling into the comfort of an assured future.

It should not have been Lewis...

The words bit Hamish's memory, and he folded the paper roughly before tossing it to the edge of the table. No. He had a plan. He would not take that path.

'Excuse me, my lord.' One of the waiters held out a card on a silver tray. 'A table of gents in the next room have invited you to join them for whist.'

More curious than flattered, Hamish followed the waiter into the next room, where he was directed to three men clustered around a square table. All of them were variations on his father: grey hair, black suits, superior expressions. As they introduced themselves, he tried to fasten their names to memory, but they were all so similar in dress and mannerisms, that he struggled to remember which was the Viscount Wiltshire and which was the Baron of Leicester. Or was it *Viscount* Leicester? Only their facial hair differed, and Hamish found himself internally referring to them as Mutton chops, Grizzly, and Walrus.

Grizzly threw down a two of spades. 'And what of your plans while in London, Dalton?'

'The usual.' Hamish rearranged his cards. 'Make calls. Attend parliament. Find a wife.'

'Not sitting in your father's seat, are you?' Mutton chops asked as he picked up the two and discarded a five.

Hamish barked out a laugh. 'Not at all. I am to *familiarise* myself with the activities of the house. But nothing more.'

'Any young lady caught your eye?' Walrus surveyed his cards. 'There have been some lovely debutantes this season.'

The silhouette of his neighbour, coupled with her high, light laughter and teasing tone, echoed in Hamish's memory before he pushed it aside. 'I only arrived in town yesterday evening. Hardly time to make a betrothal.'

'The young Lady Miranda Tatton is making an impression,' Mutton chops spoke with a light ease. 'Her mother, the viscountess, is hosting a garden party next week. I'll arrange an invite for you.'

'Lady Miranda? She sings like a vulture and can never remember if she's dancing a waltz or a polka.' Walrus pointed an accusing finger across the table. 'You only made the suggestion to keep her away from your son.'

'Preposterous. My son has simply set his sights elsewhere. Besides, the young lady has an impressive dowry,' Mutton chops said.

'And an arse to envy a caboose,' Walrus muttered to Hamish.

Hamish stifled a groan. 'I would like some help, although not on matrimonial issues. I would like to call on my Aunt Matilda, but my father seems to have misplaced her address. Can any of you gents help?'

They all shuffled in their chairs. Walrus rearranged his cards. Grizzly gave a dry cough.

Hamish looked between the three of them. No one met his gaze.

'Goodness, the time. I have an appointment. Enjoy your stay in London, lad.' Grizzly threw his cards to the table, and in a similar display of excuses and farewells, the other two stood and disappeared before Hamish had half risen to bid them good day. He slumped back into his chair.

'She's still in London.' The pronouncement came from a man sitting at a nearby table. He spoke with a slight accent. Not French. Maybe Spanish? His impeccably styled hair shone, and while clean, his suit had the worn edges of age and constant mending that Hamish recognised from having worn cast-offs for so many years. The man's dark eyes twinkled beneath a pair of bushy eyebrows, and a sliver of a smile appeared beneath a neat moustache. An impoverished gent, likely, or a common man playing at being a gent. 'And they know where she lives.'

'I gathered as much. Although, for men so terrible at bluffing, they still seem to have bested me. I'm down three shillings.'

The man pulled out a chair and took a seat at the table, and while Hamish thought to object at the overt familiarity, he was also curious. The facial hair trio reminded him of the path he could go along with, while this man teased at the edges of that alternative route, like the Cheshire Cat tempting Alice deeper into the forest. The man retrieved a thin gold cigarette case from his coat pocket, clipped it open and held it out to Hamish. Hamish shook his head. Tobacco reminded him too much of the cantankerous old bastard he'd left behind.

'Why the interest in Miss Tilly?' the man asked.

Hamish raised a brow. 'Lady Matilda Dalton is my aunt.'

The man chortled. 'Lady Matilda? You are a braver man than me to call her by her title. She insists on being called Miss Tilly. Hosts the most splendid parties.' He took a portable pen and a card from the inside of his jacket, but as he began to write, a large blob of black ink leeched out. Muttering a curse under his breath, he blotted it with a corner of the tablecloth before continuing to scrawl. He blew lightly across the card's surface until the ink shifted from shiny to matte. Satisfied that it had dried, he extended it between two fingers, but when Hamish reached for it, the man flicked the card back into his palm.

'Surely, such important knowledge deserves a little compensation?' The man tilted his head towards the waiter.

Hamish had heard of men who managed to secure memberships to clubs and spent their days mooching drinks and taking small wins at cards in lieu of applying themselves to more useful employment. He'd clearly stumbled upon one of those.

Hamish nodded at the waiter. 'Whatever he likes.'

He gave a nod and disappeared. Clearly the staff knew what the mystery man's preferred tipple was.

Hamish took the card, then flicked his watch open. Mayfair. He could walk from here and return before raising the carriage driver's suspicions.

'Is there a discrete exit?' he asked.

'I wouldn't be here otherwise.' The man pointed over his shoulder. 'Slip the waiter with blonde hair a shilling. He's been known to help a gent avoid an awkward interaction.'

Hamish lifted his hat. The man raised his glass. 'Until next time, my lord.'

The brass knocker echoed eerily against the mid-morning hustle of the tree-lined street, which was one of the slimmer avenues through Mayfair. A young, rather handsome butler opened the door. His aunt had traded in old James then. Hamish stepped into the entrance and gave the man his card. 'She's expecting you?' he asked as he closed the door.

'No, but she'll want to see me.' The butler looked to a side table by the door where three other calling cards had already been left. 'I'm her nephew,' he explained.

The butler gave him a glare that suggested this information made things worse, not better. He placed the card on a silver tray before stepping beneath an archway into the hall and making his way up the stairs.

Hamish's skin prickled with nerves and excitement. If his father knew he had come to call on his aunt, he would summon him back to the estate immediately. Even mentioning Aunt Matilda sent the old man into a tirade. Her portrait had been banished to the attic when Hamish was nine, and while he had never been privy to all the details behind their rift, he had heard rumours—rumours seemingly confirmed by his aunt's splendid villa. Supposedly, when she was younger, she had refused to marry a man of the earl's choosing, so he had cut off her allowance. Instead of capitulating, his aunt had abandoned both her allowance and dowry and become a kept woman to a carefully curated selection of nobles and wealthy merchants. Over time, she had positioned herself at the meeting point of genteel London and its dark underside. Shunned by most, tolerated by some, and embraced by a few, she didn't flaunt her choice, but nor did she hide it. And to the earl, that was unforgivable.

'Miss Tilly will see you,' said the butler.

As Hamish trudged up the stairs, elation and dread rolled in his stomach like a ship caught between squalls. One moment he surged with the determination to finally put his plan into action, in the next, he felt certain his idea was nonsense and he would simply attend a few balls, negotiate an appropriate wife, and return home to fulfil his lordly duties.

Break free. Obey. Break free. Obey.

He vacillated between options with each step on the stairs, and by the time he reached the landing, Hamish thought he might pitch his breakfast into a large Greek ewer by the door. Once announced, he stepped into the room ready to greet the woman he had not seen in twelve years. He cleared his throat, but before he could speak, he was swept into an embrace as his aunt pulled him tight against her chest.

'Hamish! Oh heavens, look at you! You're so tall, has it really been so long?' She pushed back, grasped him by his wrists and tugged him to the window. 'Let me look at you in proper light. So handsome! Your father was not the sharpest tool, but he had his head screwed on right when he married your mother. Oh my, I never thought I'd see you again.'

Hamish blinked a few times to clear his eyes and steady himself from the typhoon of emotion that washed over him. 'It's good to see you too, Lady Matilda.'

'Don't be ridiculous, call me Aunt Tilly. I won't answer to anything else.'

In Hamish's memory, his aunt had been a resplendent tower of glimmer and glitter, sparkling with gems and swishing with silks, her laughter bright and refracting through rooms like light through crystal. Now, even though he stood almost a foot taller than her, the petite woman swathed in brilliant indigo velvet, her honey-coloured hair fixed with pins and bedecked with jewelled butterflies and bees, was somehow more magnificent than the one in his memory.

'This calls for a celebration. Champagne!' Aunt Tilly called to the butler who had not moved from the door. 'Unless you would rather tea?' she asked, her tone probing.

His father would have ordered tea. 'Champagne sounds perfect.'

Aunt Tilly clapped her hands, beaming. 'Excellent. Now sit, sit. You must tell me *everything*.'

The last time Hamish had seen his aunt had been at the funerals, which she had refused to be banished from, and stood the sole woman amid a sea of stalwart men. His father had not acknowledged his estranged sister, and following his lead, no one else had either.

Hamish's life since that day had been so dreary. His aunt's eyes bubbled with expectation, but as he began to talk, he saw the enthusiasm wither once she realised just how tedious his youth had been. He spoke of the brief semester at Oxford that had been cut short when his father took a turn, and how his education had continued in the library. He made brief mention of visits to neighbours who bored him, and he hinted at affairs with their lonely wives. The tennis in summer. Just the two of them each Christmas. And no chance for the travels or adventures he had dreamt of when young, because all his time was spent at his father's side receiving instruction. By the end of his story, his heart scraped raw, and the familiar anger burned in his stomach.

'I take it the years have not softened him?' Aunt Tilly's voice had lost its vivacity. There was no explaining a man like the earl, and like him, his aunt knew the cut of his righteousness. She circled a finger over the mouth of her empty champagne flute, and the crystal sang into their shared sadness. 'Hamish, why are you here?'

'I have been sent to London to find a wife, "no lower than a viscount's daughter," so that I may carry on the Dalton legacy.'

'Not in London. Why are you *here*.' Aunt Tilly took the champagne bottle by the neck and sloshed an inch into her glass, before reaching forward and upending the last few drops into his. 'He would not allow you to see a family disgrace like me unless I repented, which I have no intention of doing. And while many will turn a blind eye to one visit, if you make my company a habit, you'll be unlikely to have a baron's scullery maid look your way. I am so happy to see you, but if you think you can call on me without consequences, you are being painfully naive.'

Hamish stared into the half inch in his flute, a few lazy bubbles clinging to the side. In the past few hours, he'd experienced more love and warmth than he had in more than a decade. Even his aunt's warning to keep his distance came from compassion, not contempt.

'About six months ago, he got sick,' he began, trying to hold his voice steady. 'Almost everyone in the county got sick. Three staff died. In the village, entire households were lost. Typhoid.' Hamish stared into the fire, the embers a reminder of the heat that had burned through the damp rag he had pressed to his father's forehead. 'I sat by his side, as I'd sat for years, terrified the disease would take him because I believed everything he said. That I wasn't ready. That I would be lost without him. And in a fever dream, can you imagine what he said?'

Tilly gave a small, almost imperceptible shake of her head.

'It should not have been Lewis.' Hamish tried but failed to keep the venom from his voice. 'It should have been you.'

'Oh, Hamish. Don't you think on it, he isn't worth it. Find a lady who makes you happy and live your own life.'

'No. I won't bring home a wife to suffer through him. Or worse, have a child to be his favourite or his kicking ball. I came here because I need your help. All he cares about is the Dalton name. His legacy. Well, I want to drag his name, his damned precious *legacy* through the mud. I am going to be the season's biggest scandal.' Hamish threw back the last of his champagne and set the glass down. 'Aunt Tilly, I want you to make me a rake.'

Aunt Tilly stared hard, her eyes full of surprise. He forced himself to hold her stare as his heart thumped with anger and anticipation, readying himself for her objections. But instead, her lips twitched, then she threw back her head and laughed. 'Rakes and scoundrels aren't made, they just are. My sweet boy, you don't have it in you.'

'I do!' he snapped, aware he sounded like an indignant child, but he was too full of emotion to temper his tone. 'I can be a rake. I can do rakish things.'

'Prove it,' she said. 'Throw some insult into the street.'

'At whom?' he asked.

'At anyone. You're a rake. You don't care.'

Hamish pushed himself from the chair and crossed the room in a few strides before opening the window. The smell of horse manure and smoke rushed in. The street teemed with men transporting goods, as drays, small carts, and the odd carriage lumbered along. Women barked orders at tailing children, and a newspaper boy shouted the day's headlines. Close by the house, a labourer with a bag stuffed with coal slung over one shoulder trudged past. 'You there,' Hamish called. The man paused and turned a soot-stained face upward. 'You're a mess. Go... go wash up, why don't you.' Hamish pulled the window closed, crossed his arms across his chest and leaned back against the plate. 'Like that?'

'Oh, that poor man,' Tilly covered her mouth with her hand. 'I think I hear him crying.'

'You do?' Hamish pushed the window open and looked down to the street, an apology on his lips.

Aunt Tilly chuckled. 'My advice, nephew? Find some docile wife who will be grateful to share your title, set up a mistress in that old townhouse, and pretend that keeping two women makes you interesting, like every other noble with a fat purse and a member that still salutes. Forget your father.'

'Forget him? The man is stamped on every corner of my life. I gave him everything. Nothing will ever be enough, no wife, no heir, or me.' Hamish crossed back to the fireplace, buttoned his coat, and snatched his hat from the table. 'If you won't help me, I'll determine a course myself. I've heard stories from travellers and read enough in the papers. I'll go to Haymarket and drink my allowance away with some woman of the night on my arm.'

'Woman of the night? Heaven, help me,' Tilly mumbled under her breath. 'You won't last a week. Fine, I'll help you.'

Hamish tried to stop a grin from cracking, instead tilting his head to give his aunt what he hoped was a devilishly rakish smile. 'My thanks, gracious lady.'

She rolled her eyes and waved him away. 'Be back here, Tuesday next week, eleven o'clock sharp. And Hamish,' she called just before he took his leave. 'Wear your best suit.'

Chapter Four

On the wall at the far end of Iris's office, reaching ten feet wide and eight feet high, Papa's dear friend Jonah Worthington had painted a map of the world. Unlike the maps printed in her schoolbooks and almanacs, it wasn't marked with the red blotches of the British Empire as footprints across the world, but instead showed patches of jungle green forest, sandy yellow deserts, coal black mountains, squiggly blue rivers, and, amazingly, so much aqua ocean.

This room had been her playroom when she was a child, not that she spent much time at inside play. For her nineteenth birthday, her father had transformed it into something more fitting a young woman. The hopping bunnies and green-eyed cats had been painted over with soft cream walls and chocolate brown trim, the dollhouse and children's furniture had been removed and, in their place, her father had installed a wide cedar desk and a bookshelf so tall she had to stand on tiptoe to reach the uppermost shelf.

'That's only part of your gift. My dear daughter,' Papa had said as he held out an envelope and gestured to the map, 'I give you the world.'

It had taken an achingly long time to open the envelope because her fingers had trembled so much, but eventually she had tugged out a ticket for the Dover to Calais steamer.

'I am going abroad to source new stock,' he had said, his voice soft, and she knew he was trying to temper his excitement. 'And I understand if you would rather stay. Join some society, maybe start courting. You have every ability you need to make your own choice about your path ahead. But nothing would make me happier than if you would join me on my next journey.'

Almost a full year had passed since Hamish had left. Her letters had gone unanswered, and the townhouse remained dormant. The thought of another year of balls, tittering women, and men who pawed her waist when her father wasn't looking, made her nauseous. Her father offered not only a chance to see the world, but also to escape the confines of Honeysuckle Street, where every step held some memory of Hamish. Why should she be tortured when he had so easily forgotten her?

And so, she had begun her informal apprenticeship into Abberton Trading, later renamed Abberton and Co when they had expanded to take on investors and form the board. On each journey she and Papa went on, they had posed for calotype photographs and, where they could, collected *cartes postales*. She kept entrance tickets, coins and notes, and when they returned from their travels, Iris had fixed her souvenirs to the map with pins and paste. Over time, the wall had been covered with mementoes from almost every continent, and her map had become a keepsake album where she revisited her memories not by sitting and flipping pages, but by walking and reaching and touching.

Iris rubbed her thumb against the thick edge of a photograph that showed Papa and her astride camels with the sphinx looming behind them. They had found the most extraordinary tiles in Egypt, although a crate had cracked when they had been dropped too roughly onto the pier. She walked her fingers over the map until they reached a card pinned by Venice, where they had sourced beads and lace, and then across the ocean to America, where they had investigated new developments in farm machinery. On that trip, almost three years ago, she had thought of Hamish and, on a whim, bought a card of the Union Aqueduct to send back to the Caplin House. Always better with numbers, she'd resisted the impulse to write the words that itched at her fingers, and instead scrawled, *The Union Aqueduct is 220 feet long. Extraordinary, don't you think?*

A tap and a meow came from the window. Iris scrubbed her palm over her eyes to dismiss the memories she'd allowed herself to be drawn into, then crossed the room and pushed the window sash up.

'You are a cad, Spencer,' she said as the grey tom leapt onto the floor and flopped into an unlikely shaft of sunlight. Completely nonplussed by her name calling, he contorted himself and began to lick his hind leg.

Iris lowered herself into the chair behind her desk, before flipping through the stack of correspondence in front of her. Mostly tiresome letters to her father from businesses who wished to engage with Abberton and Co but did not want to meet their conditions. *I cannot secure the necessary labour. The workdays are too short to meet demand. An adult cannot fit beneath the machines.* Feeble excuses, she knew, but all requiring a response, if only to make clear that if they wanted access to the Abberton network they had to commit to their terms. The government was already bringing in legislation to improve working conditions, and Papa had always prided himself on being ahead of the government. The men who had built their profits on long days and children's fingers would find themselves out of pocket the longer they resisted.

Iris flicked the folder closed. Normally, such correspondence suited her, the replies flowing hot from her outraged mind to her fingers, but the earlier visit from Mr Sanders kept invading her thoughts. Once again, he had been evasive and hadn't told her about problems that Papa had always let her help solve.

Iris nudged Spencer with a foot. He grumbled but did not move, although he sprang to attention when Gena entered the room with the tea tray, his eyes shifting to the milk jug balanced beside the pot.

'Mason said to tell you, your father is reading that atlas you bought him last Christmas. He's got an extra blanket and is happy enough.' Gena set the tray down and placed a cup and saucer before Iris. Instead of taking the tray and leaving, she made slow work of circling the room with a cloth, wiping at dust that wasn't there. 'Is there anything else, miss? Is the tea strong enough? It was quite an exciting morning.'

'Out with it,' Iris said, trying to keep her tone level. She could almost picture the rest of the staff huddled at the base of the stairs, straining to overhear the conversation. Jonah's starving artists made loyal workers, and never would they breathe a word of gossip outside of the house, but that didn't mean they didn't gossip amongst themselves.

Iris's mother had been one of them, although, of the staff, only Gena had known her. Her mother had once been an artist's model, posing as Diana, goddess of the hunt, for Jonah, who had found her pregnant and begging on the streets of Soho after Iris's father, her blood father, had been lost at sea. Heartbroken, her mother hadn't survived her birth. While many a man would have sent a hungry mouth to the orphanage, when he heard the story, Albert Abberton had instead adopted her, hired a wetnurse, and announced in a small notice in the paper that he now had a daughter named Iris. She had a strange connection, and disconnection, to the staff, aware that it could have been her serving tea instead of waiting for its delivery. They were family, yet not. Friends, yet in her employ. Iris always felt an uncomfortable gap between worlds that she never quite knew how to straddle. Perhaps that was why she'd always been so close to Hamish when they were young. The pair of them had found ways to adjust, although they never quite fit. Only when they were together did they make sense.

Gena wiped her cloth across the windowpane. 'We were just wondering if you'll tell Mr Sanders about Mr Abberton? About his condition and all?'

'Tell Mr Sanders? He can't even bear to leave a message with me, a *woman*. He would implode with shock if he knew I'd been keeping the books and submitting reports.'

Papa had always said they would tell the board about her work once they were more comfortable with one another, which she took to mean they would tell them a woman helped run the company once they saw the return on their investment. But he had started to slip just as the company had started to grow, and to compensate, she had taken on more work, not realising the clock had been against them. Every day the hope that he might return to his old self faded a little more. Now, she walked a razor, trying to conceal his memory loss while needing to stay involved lest the board steer their carefully planned expansion off course, but also drowning under the mountains of work that they had once shared.

Gena stopped pretending to dust and turned to Iris, her eyes full of concern. 'Maybe, if you tell him right, he could help you. Be an ally. I've known you since you were a babe, and I hate to see you working so hard and missing the joy of life. And if you can forgive me for saying, it's not what your father wanted for you. Maybe this annual meeting thing could be a chance to let them know.'

'They would take over all of this.' Iris waved her hand across the mounds of paper and notes on the table. 'And I will be left with nothing more complicated than the weekly shopping. They don't understand. They will ruin everything Papa and I worked for. Our dreams.'

'Your father wouldn't have brought them on if he thought them so incompetent. You could step back. Travel again. Or maybe find a husband. Even at thirty, you're still pretty enough.'

'I'm only twenty-nine,' Iris muttered.

'Even better.' Gena chirped, before her voice dropped low. 'You always wanted a family when you were younger. Isn't that why you pestered your father to let you debut? Now, all you do is work. I'm just not sure how much of this is about him, and how much is you not wanting to let go.'

Iris leaned back in her chair a little, twisting in the seat to look across the large cedar desk where she had sat opposite her father as they kept the books, sourced stock, and planned adventures.

'Why not take a break?' Gena continued. 'Enjoy the season a little. Mr Hamish is back in town, and you two were always quite the pair. You could have some fun.'

Iris's gaze settled on the townhouse across the vacant block. One of the maids had thrown open the window and now leaned out and shook a dusting cloth in the air. It had been Hamish's window. She could always spot it, because it was the same window she had thrown pebbles at late at night, and he would climb down and meet her in the dilapidated ruin of Number 6. By firelight in the cellar, they told ghost stories, or on the nights they were too tired for imagination, read from a book by the light of a tallow candle snuck from the kitchen.

'He's Lord Dalton now,' Iris snapped. 'He won't have time for me.'

'Spend some time with your father, then. You work like the devil. More than he and you put together before he was on the board.'

Iris sat up a little straighter, then rummaged through a stack of papers until she found a sheet wedged into a folder labelled, *Annual General Meeting – May 1873*. They had discussed the terms for electing a new board member, when Mr Sanders had been nominated to take over from his uncle who had fallen ill.

Iris flicked open the folder and ran her finger down the meeting minutes until she found a reference to the boards constitution.

Item 6. All changes to the composition of the board must be agreed on by a majority by the board.

'That's it!' Iris slammed the folder onto the desk.

Gena startled. 'You'll tell Mr Sanders?' she asked, her cloth poised mid-air.

'Most certainly not. I have an ally on the board already. Papa is still on the board. I'll have Papa write a letter, telling them he's retiring and nominating me to take his place. It says here, if in agreement, the board can appoint a new member. They'll have no choice but to vote me on.'

Iris pulled a sheet of paper towards her, took up her father's old pen, and began to write:

I have been considering retirement for some time and would like to propose my daughter Miss Iris Abberton to take my place on the board. I will teach her everything I know.

'So, you won't be telling Mr Sanders? Stepping back a little?' Gena said, her voice a mixture of confusion and disappointment.

'Now is the time to strike, Gena, not rest on our laurels.' Iris sipped at her tea. The black bitterness slid lukewarm down her throat. She set the cup aside and continued to write as Gena took the tray to the door. 'Leave Spencer the milk. He hasn't taken his eyes from the jug since you came in.'

CHAPTER FIVE

It wasn't big things, but seemingly inconsequential things that sparked Hamish's recollections and sent a flurry of memories ricocheting through him. The slant of the sun across the ceiling reminded him of all the mornings he had laid in bed and planned a day's adventures. The branch scratching on his window when the wind got up brought forth recollections of scrunching into a ball of fear when one of Iris's ghost stories nibbled at his nerves. In a world so unfamiliar it could have been a foreign country, these slivers pounded with stark familiarity.

When young, Hamish had often climbed out his window early to make a short prowl of the surrounding streets, in the hopes of concocting some scheme he could bring back to Iris when they inevitably met up. The past two days he had picked up the routine again, although now he used the front door, and instead of scurrying between shadows, he rode his bay mare at a leisurely pace. And instead of climbing the tree to tap on Iris's window, he looked across the vacant block and thought about paying her a visit, before finally tearing himself away to run some errand.

How did one approach an old friend after twelve years?

Hamish slowed from a trot to a walk as he turned onto Honeysuckle Street. Almost a week had passed since his visit to his aunt, and since then, he had spent his days making calls as dictated by his father. Last night, his first evening without a dinner invitation, he had rattled through the townhouse, both craving company and relishing a freedom he hadn't known since before the accident. The house had been kept in good order, although without his mother's commitment to maintain appearances, nothing had been updated since his youth. He had grown used to her and Lewis's absence at the estate, as their belongings had been gradually packed away, sold, or otherwise moved on. Walking through Number 8 felt more like looking at a painting where his mother and Lewis had been hastily removed, leaving turpentine smudges in the oil, while the surrounding image remained untouched. In odd moments, he half expected to enter the breakfast room and find his mother seated at the table picking at toast, or in the evenings, to stumble upon Lewis and his father smoking pipes by the fire. Grief and envy weighed in equal measure as he remembered the trio of his parents and their favourite son, and once again he felt like a spectator in his own family.

While Number 8 had remained frozen inside, the outside world had barely paused to show a moment of pity for the Dalton tragedy before it moved on. The industry of soot and smoke pervaded almost everywhere, and on foggy days, was brought low to the ground. The miasmic stench that his parents once fretted over had been secreted beneath the city and into a fantastic labyrinth of pipes and tunnels, taking the waste of the bulging population and sending it out of sight. Construction and progress splattered London, reshaping some places and leaving others untouched.

Honeysuckle Street was a similar mix of evolution and stagnation. At first, he had only the capacity to take in the erasure of Number 6, but each day he rode, he was able to appreciate other changes more thoroughly. The uneven row of mismatched houses on the opposite side of the street had been replaced with five Belgrave townhouses. The repetition of façades jarred him, as the only distinction between each home was a different coloured front door. Irving, always happy to pass on the cook's knowledge as he helped him shave each morning, had provided a brief overview of his neighbours. Number 1, with a green door, was home to Mr Babbage, a clerk or similar at a bank, who was engaged in a long running feud with Mr Hempel in Number 3. Hamish knew of the Hempels—they had been residents when he was young. When Hamish had left, Mrs Hempel had been pregnant, with a baby on her waist and a toddler at her feet. Now, twelve years later, she appeared with the same rounded stomach and a toddler still grasping her skirts. A steady stream of older children came and went each day on foot, or by bicycle, whether to school or employment, Irving didn't know. Mrs Crofts, the curtain twitching, stubborn old bag in Number 5 who had always tried to catch Iris and him at mischief, had also remained. Had she moved out of the way for them to build the row, or had they constructed around her? Meanwhile, an antiquarian lady and her ward occasionally emerged from a bright blue door at Number 7, while Number 9 remained dark and uninhabited. Perhaps the house belonged to a country family who had not come to London this year, or maybe it was a rental between tenants.

Next, Hamish passed Miss Delaney's large palatial villa, which was clad in white stucco and fronted by Doric columns. It appeared almost garish next to the earthy brown brick and stone of the Abberton house. He refrained from allowing his gaze to linger on Number 4, and, instead, turned his sights towards home. From his vantage, and without Number 6, the Ashlar façade and cheap brick of the Dalton house was dwarfed by Number 10, the four-story sandstone villa that sheltered behind a high wrought iron fence. His grace's home sat aloof from the rest of the street, much like the young man who had become a duke before his sixth birthday.

'You would wait a week before coming to call on me, Lord Dalton? Shame on you.'

Startled, Hamish looked down on the svelte form of a dazzlingly beautiful woman. Clad in a silk mauve dress with a plunging neckline, she looked up at him, but the bold anger in her pale blue eyes soon had him swinging off his horse and bowing his greeting in repentance. She had moved onto the street when Hamish was fifteen, and then, she'd glowed as a youthful beauty, barely twenty-one, and hailed as an operatic angel. Time had not dimmed her perfection, and judging by her tone, had not batted her determination either. 'My apologies, Miss Delaney,' Hamish stammered. 'I had calls to make on behalf of my father.'

Miss Odette Delaney, famed soprano of the stage, rumoured lover of dukes and princes, casually clasped his biceps and kissed first one cheek, then the other, in the French style, before raising a disapproving eyebrow. 'And I would not be on his list, would I?'

'Well, you see...' Hamish rubbed the back of his head. 'No. No you weren't.'

She chuckled. '*Bien.*' Miss Delaney smirked, then looked to the stairs that led to the front door of Number 4. 'Iris, darling,' she called, a slight song to her voice. 'Do you remember Lord Dalton, our neighbour?'

Six stairs led the way to the Abberton front door, and Hamish dragged his eyes forcibly over each one, his eyes tunnelling each groove in both anticipation and dread. He took in his first clear view of Iris Abberton as she stepped out of her front door, accompanied by her father. His stomach tightened, and his lungs lost breath.

Without the interference of a fog, there was little to reconcile the lady before him with the stringy girl from his memory. The woman who steadily guided Mr Abberton could have been an older sister, but not Iris. The bright fire of her hair had mellowed to copper, and the tangle of curls had been smoothed and restrained, covered by an innocent white floral bonnet. The straight lines of her body had filled, and he had seduced enough women to know that beneath the demure high collar and nipped waist were sumptuous curves and legs long enough to wrap around his hips. The freckles that had stippled her nose and cheeks had faded, and while her lips were fuller, when they turned up at the corners, the smile didn't show her teeth or reach her eyes.

She focused completely on her father, watching his feet as he took the stairs at a steady pace. Their easy affection had always stoked a slight envy in Hamish. Abberton loved his daughter fiercely, like she was his own, while Hamish could barely manage a smile from his father despite the obvious family resemblance.

'Of course, I remember Lord Dalton.' Iris hadn't looked up from assisting her father, and likely hadn't seen Miss Delaney gesture in his direction. 'Lord La-di-dah, although he seems to have forgotten everyone except Spencer. He has not sent a card or paid a call on anyone in the street, not even his grace. I imagine he will move onto better accommodation soon enough. Something a bit more *lordly*.'

'I don't know. It's a terribly convenient location, even despite the lack of lordliness,' he said with half a grin.

Iris's head snapped up. 'Hamish—I mean, Lord Dalton.' She had reached the street, and crossed the few steps to him haltingly, her dark grey wool gown billowing a little as she walked. She held out her hand and gave a short bob.

Hamish took her hand, clad in her soft kid gloves. 'Please accept my apologies, Miss Abberton. I have been somewhat busy since I arrived. I should have sent a note, but every day I told myself I would make the short journey to your door, but every day threw up different obligations.'

'It is lovely to see you, and to find you looking less fluffy.' Her eyes darted over his suit, and her lips twitched into half a smirk.

'I can't believe that feline demon is still alive,' he said, squeezing her fingers.

'Alive and building an empire. He has a new lady love every other month.'

'Every other month? Perhaps I should seek his advice,' Hamish said with a chuckle, then pulled back, embarrassed, and released her while chiding himself for having made such a crass joke. 'My apologies, miss. I have been in the country too long.'

And just like that, her lips twitched again as a smile cracked, this time so rich and full it reached her eyes. She giggled, and while he knew it was more at his awkwardness than his joke, he still found her laughter the lightest, most delightful escape from her lips. In less than a heartbeat, he was back in the park climbing trees to steal feathers from birds' nests or sending tremors across the pond to make the ducks take flight and upset a temperance society picnic.

'There's a sound I have not heard in an age,' Miss Delaney said. 'Laughter from Iris. You should have called sooner, my lord.'

'What brings you to London after all this time?' Iris asked, a sharpness cutting across the word *time*.

He thought about spinning some lie, but as he inhaled a deception, he caught a slight eyebrow raise from Iris, and he knew she would have already deduced his father's instructions. Her mind had always been quick, and really, there was only one reason why a man his age, and without a seat in parliament, returned to town after so long away. Best to get it out. 'My father has suggested I begin searching for a wife.'

'Well, London is the place for that,' she quipped.

He couldn't say why her speedy response chaffed, and yet, it did. Was she courting someone, perhaps that Mr Sanders? Or did she not bother with courtship and simply had lovers placed at her convenience? Sick envy spread. Not so much at images of other men claiming her body, although his gut twisted at the thought. But that in his absence, she may have found someone new to whisper her secrets to. He had never divulged anything more intimate than his thoughts on the weather to any woman, save her.

'Hamish Dalton? Well, I never. Haven't been in my kitchen, have you?' Mr Abberton crossed the path, waving a finger in the air.

'Mr Abberton,' Hamish held out his hand. 'It's a pleasure to see you.'

'You recognise Lord Dalton?' As her father approached, the furrows on Iris's brow smoothed, and then that smile, her proper smile, lit up her face. 'He remembers you.'

'Always stealing biscuits this one,' Mr Abberton continued. 'Not that it showed! Always a runt. And forever running amok in the streets with my daughter.' He put his hand on his belly and laughed before turning to Odette. 'If you have daughters, don't let him near them. He'll have them climbing trees and chasing ducks through the park.'

Mr Abberton and Miss Delaney had always been firm friends—why would he address her like she was a stranger? Hamish turned to Miss Delaney, and then Iris. Iris's smile fell. Miss Delaney gave an awkward cough. Mr Abberton continued to stare at Hamish, until a mist filled his eyes and the recognition faded.

'Come Papa.' Iris threaded her hand around his elbow. 'We had better start for Miss Delaney's before the weather turns.' She gave him her half-smile along with another bob. 'Good day, my lord.'

Hamish watched as the two of them strolled down the path. There had been an old man on the estate like Mr Abberton. Forgetful at first, the sort of thing people laughed and shook their heads over. Then he would forget work he had promised to do, despite never having done so before. Then he forgot his wife's name, and eventually his own, until he slipped into a grey shadow of himself. Iris's father had been one of the sharpest, most self-assured men Hamish had known. It was one of the things that rankled the old earl, that a self-made man would dare to live on the same street as nobility and never try to emulate them. Not that it ever seemed to bother the duke next door, only Hamish's father. The same affliction that had taken the old man on the estate from his family seemed to have found Iris's father, and Hamish felt cold and angry at the unjustness of it.

'We would appreciate it if you would keep your observations to yourself.' Miss Delaney spoke in a low, but firm, tone. 'Many would suggest he be moved to Bedlam if they knew. Iris has enough to carry right now.'

'Wouldn't things be easier for her, if he was somewhere where he could be cared for?' he asked.

She fixed him with a penetrating glare. 'Would they?'

They were maybe twenty feet away when Iris turned back. 'Hamish—I mean, Lord Dalton.'

'Hamish, please,' he said. 'Anything else from you sounds odd.'

She smiled again, another proper smile. 'We are going to Covent Garden tomorrow night for the opera. Miss Delaney has arranged us a box. Papa never misses opening night. You seem to have helped his memory. Would you care to join us?'

Hamish gave a small nod. 'I would be delighted.'

'Wonderful. Come to the house at seven o'clock. We can share a carriage.'

Hamish doffed his hat. 'I look forward to it.'

Hamish bid farewell to Miss Delaney, and by the time he had vaulted onto his horse, the three of them had already made it to the end of the street. The sun split the clouds, and golden rays lit on the diamonds and rubies the soprano wore as she made her way up the curved stairs to her villa, and combined with her flowing silk gown, she sparkled against the London drizzle like a rainbow. In comparison, Iris, in her grey wool and flannel, could have been the clouds that blanketed the sky. But as he watched his old friend guide her father, something he said made her laugh. Her soft pink lips pulled back to show straight white teeth, her cheeks glowed soft pink, joy inched into her brilliant emerald eyes, and she instantly transformed into the sun itself. Miss Delaney was a beauty, but always far too dazzling for him to comprehend, too much like his aunt to inspire any attraction or lust. But seeing Iris just as she was, sent his heart into a staccato. For a moment he stayed lost, confused by the transformation of the wild girl he had grown up with into the monochrome woman she had become. A burst of memory exploded in his mind's eye. Her laying back against his coat, her red hair spilling behind her, arms outstretched, thighs splaying, before her fingers dug into his back, and her whimpers caressing his ear.

'Oh Iris,' he muttered to himself. 'Why did we have to grow up?'

CHAPTER SIX

The last notes hung in the air, the audience holding its collective breath in rapture. As the vibrations from the orchestra pit faded, the opera house filled with thrumming ovation, followed by cheers and shouts of 'Bravo!' Papa pushed himself to his feet, clapping furiously before wiping a tear from his cheek. Odette's performance had been spectacular, and as the curtain inched down, Iris was sure their neighbour blew a kiss in their direction. When Papa walked to the edge of the box, Hamish leaned across the vacant seat and spoke in a slightly raised voice that Iris could just hear over the applause.

'The show is much better from up here,' he said with a wink and a glance at the stalls.

Iris laughed. 'And to stay until the end.'

Once, they had snuck in and watched three songs before they were discovered and bundled back into the street. Iris cursed the flutter in her chest at the thought that Hamish remembered that day.

Like most of their adventures, it had started as a dare, which was pointless as they always wound up doing everything together. Goading one another on, they had dodged the ushers and slunk through the shadows, just to see how far they could go. In the stalls, the gaslights from the stage had spilled into the audience, and a soft yellow had lit the defined angles of Hamish's jaw, made pools of his deep brown eyes, and caressed the mischievous dimple that sat tucked in his cheek. He had watched the stage; she had watched him. With Verdi's *Il trovatore* swirling around them, Iris had realised that the excitement she felt when the Dalton carriage rattled by was more than just the thrill of her playmate returning, a feeling she'd maybe always known but had been too scared to interrogate. After the season had ended, and the Dalton family had returned to the country, she had pestered her father into letting her debut, had begged for a lady's maid to help her learn how to style her hair, and ordered a new wardrobe. She had brimmed with the innocent hope that, when he returned, he might see her differently, too.

How naive she had been.

Iris tucked her hand into her father's elbow, and with Hamish beside her, they moved towards the landing. He used a different cologne now, something spicier than orange water, undercut with a hint of rosemary and mint. His scent pressed against her as they bunched together, intoxicatingly new. In the press her foot caught on her hem, and she lurched uneasily until his arm wrapped around her waist. His hand splayed, his firm palm pressing against her torso, the end of each finger imprinting against her. With a slight jerk, he drew her close against him, until she tugged her dress free and planted her feet on the carpet.

'Apologies.' The word exhaled over her nape, its warmth curling over her exposed skin, while the pressure of his hand lingered, spurring those damn butterflies into a frenzy. 'Would you like to stay for supper?' he asked.

'Do you always think about food?' she said, trying to cover the catch in her voice.

'Not always.' He grinned. 'Sometimes, I sleep.'

Iris looked to her father. Music always seemed to help his mood and his memory, and tonight, he was in good spirits. 'Maybe a small glass of wine? I don't like to keep Papa out too late.'

'A small wine?' Hamish watched her, confusion in his eyes, before he gave her a delicious grin. 'Do you remember when we drank that bottle of my father's port in the cellar of Number 6?'

Iris snorted with laughter, before coughing to cover the indelicate noise she had made. 'I thought the vein in Mrs Crofts's temple would burst when she caught us dancing in her garden.'

'Lucky Spencer came along when he did. Otherwise, I think she'd still be shrieking at us.'

The crowd thinned, and Hamish walked beside her, keeping pace with Papa's steady shuffle.

'Mr Abberton?' came a voice from behind them.

Papa spun around and stood nose to nose with Mr Sanders. Iris had never known him to talk of the opera. Why would he attend, tonight of all nights?

'May I speak with you privately? About the agenda?' Mr Sanders stared directly at Papa. Iris could have been invisible. 'I have a table, in a quiet corner. Mr Abberton, are you well?'

Papa, eyes flickering, searched Mr Sanders's face, but unlike with Hamish, there was no spark of recognition. 'Iris, who is this man?'

'Who am I?' Mr Sanders's voice rose a little with indignity. 'Sir, we know each other quite well—'

Hamish burst out laughing. 'Mr Abberton, you are a trickster.' He placed a guiding hand on Papa's shoulder. 'I smell biscuits. And pheasant. Now Albert, please continue with your story.' And before Iris could protest, Hamish had ushered Papa away and into the supper room, leaving her standing on the landing with Mr Sanders and his piercing stare.

'Who is your companion?' Mr Sanders snapped, his gaze following her father and Hamish as they moved into the supper room. 'Is he *accompanying* you?'

'Who accompanies me to the theatre is not your concern.' Iris bristled. She was in her father's company; he had no right to question her. If the police started a morality patrol, Mr Sanders would easily make sergeant. He always stood stiff and straight backed, yet at her reply, seemed to become even more angular.

'Given your father's recommendation, it is my concern. Who accompanies you may ultimately have repercussions for the company. Reputations matter. Perhaps not with the everyday man on the street who only seeks to buy a pretty trinket, but with investors it is paramount. A woman on the board is one thing, a woman with questionable associations or a spendthrift husband would be disastrous.'

'Lord Dalton is heir to Earl Caplin. He is my childhood friend, nothing more.' The words came out smoothly, even though inside, they bit. 'Let me assure you, I don't ever plan to marry. My focus is my father's company. I assumed you received his letter?'

'We did. It came as a bit of a shock. He had never mentioned you actually working with him before.'

'Well, I travelled with him since I was nineteen. I grew up watching him work. I know the company. I know what it means to him.'

'There is more to being on the board than going on trips and buying things.' Iris swallowed a retort. He made it sound like her and her father's work all those years had been nothing more than holidays and shopping. 'One must have a vision for growth. The board's vote must be unanimous. Mr Collins will likely do anything your father recommends, but Mr Vincent is slower to accept change. He may take some convincing.'

'And yourself?' Iris held his gaze, even as a small fracas sounded behind them. 'What are your views on such things?'

Mr Sanders stared down at her over his spectacles. 'I am not against a woman on the board. I am a modern man. But what I want to know is, do you have the capacity for vision? What can you offer us that we don't already have?'

Vision? She had one, an idea that she and Papa had talked over on the boat home after their last trip to Canada. They had discussed the logistics, obstacles, and opportunities of it as the wind whipped their hair and the gulls farewelled them from the harbour. Before Papa had fallen ill, she had started writing it down and calculating the resources she would need to make it work. It required only a modest investment, but the whole thing was too complex for one person to execute alone. It needed a team of intrepid souls, good partners, along with financial backing. Could this be her chance to turn that spark into reality?

'Can you manage that, Miss Abberton?' Mr Sanders said. 'A presentation of what you can bring to the company before we vote?'

Iris hated the immense swell of gratitude in her chest, but still, couldn't restrain from clasping Mr Sanders's hand, pressing her gloved palm against his and gushing, 'I have the most extraordinary business proposal. A new direction. You won't regret it, I assure you.'

Mr Sanders pulled back, clearly uncomfortable with the overt familiarity. 'Try to control your emotions. It does not suit business. You have a week. We shall see you then.'

As he moved away, a cacophony erupted behind her, a combination of raucous chortling and shocked huffs of outrage. Hamish and Papa emerged from the throng, flanked by a mixture of wide grins and frowns. On the landing, Hamish gripped his side before half bending with laughter.

Iris hurried over. 'What did you do?'

'I did nothing,' Hamish replied. 'Your father, however, told the most spectacular story. About a camel and a—'

'A flagon of sherry? Oh, good heavens, not that one.' Iris tucked her hand around her father's elbow and shot an apologetic smile at some ladies standing nearby, two of whom scowled, and one of whom hid her amusement behind her fan. 'Would you call the carriage, Hamish? I think we had better get him home.'

Mr Rogers helped Papa climb up the folding steps and into the carriage, still chuckling and humming a few notes from the show. Iris followed, wanting to tell him about the conversation she'd just had with Mr Sanders, but also knowing it would only confuse him. So much had changed since the last annual meeting, when she had helped Papa with his preparation, revised his calculations, and given him some notes on cards. In a year, would he remember her name? Would he remember his own?

He'd been so passionate about his work. He'd built something from nothing, brought the world to the everyday man and woman, and did it without grinding the people who worked for him to dust. He sponsored schools, gave money to kitchens in churches, not to mention finding work for every dejected and broken artist Jonah came across. He'd once said to her, when they were travelling across Italy, that he never sought to build an empire, only to leave the world a little better than when he came into it. And now, it was up to her to continue his legacy.

'So,' Hamish said as he settled into the opposite site of the carriage, leaning back against the squabs and crossing one boot over the other. 'How long have you been running Abberton?'

Cold fear flooded her. If Hamish had noticed as much in a day, would others infer the same? If word got out before a formal appointment, if the board knew that all this time she'd been posing as her father...

'Don't look so shocked, your secret is safe,' he continued with a smirk. 'Miss Delaney hinted that you were carrying a heavy burden, and knowing you as I do, I deduced the rest. You always were a marvel with numbers.'

Iris, balanced precariously on the edge of the seat, rested a steadying hand on the wood panelling as the carriage lurched forward. Hamish watched out the window, the soft glow of evening giving his skin a slightly sallow look, and his smug expression deepened as he flicked between shadows and light.

'As you know me?' Her cold question cut through the warmth of the carriage, almost lost under her father's gentle snores. Maybe fatigue from the evening was beginning to overwhelm her, or perhaps her patience had been worn threadbare by Mr Sanders, but Iris could not contain her annoyance any longer. 'Hamish. Don't.'

'Don't what? Tell you how marvellous you are? I won't, then. You are as dull as a work worn pencil,' he said, still not looking at her.

'Don't pretend you still know me.' Iris held tight to the edge of the seat as the carriage rounded a corner, her nails digging into the leather. Beside her, Papa gave a light snore. 'And don't pretend it meant nothing that you left.'

Hamish had always been calmer than her, but quick to anger if she found a tender spot, his sunny demeanour swirling to a storm in a blink. 'It wasn't my choice, in case you've forgotten,' he said, his voice as caustic as her own. 'You think I liked being trapped out at the estate, suddenly worth my father's attention because I might one day be earl? God Iris, I lost my mother and brother in one day.'

'I can't imagine the pain you went through. But would it have been so hard to write one letter? You were my best friend. My everything. And then you left, and you never looked back. It was like you died, too.'

The air between them fizzed with hurt and recriminations, each of them staring the other down. When she'd finally accepted that Hamish wasn't coming back to London and wasn't going to return her letters, it had taken all her resolve to blockade her feelings. He persisted as a dull ache, and like a bag slung over her shoulder that was too heavy to carry but impossible to put down, she had staggered through a street where every step held his memory. With time, she'd learnt how to juggle its weight. Between each journey with her father, she grew a little stronger. Carrying the burden became a little easier. But the suddenness of his return without so much as an apology had split her open, and every emotion she'd ever felt about him—sadness, anger, pity, and love—spilled out like a wave so tall it threatened to swamp and suffocate her. How dare he come back and try to slide in like he hadn't left, completely untouched by her absence from his life when she had felt his so keenly.

The carriage squeaked and knocked along with the sound of the wheels clattering over cobblestones. Angry fire licked Hamish's face as his ire held her own. Papa snorted into a dream, and Hamish's gaze flicked, then held.

He stayed focused on her father, his chest heaving slightly, biting his lip. His expression softened, and he bowed his head.

'At first, it was easier to just be numb. Even remembering Honeysuckle Street hurt. I wanted to travel and chase dreams, but then I was tied to the estate, desperately trying to learn everything. One day, I realised how long it had been, and staying detached seemed easier. I thought you would have moved on. Married. You were the belle of the season. Not in name, I know, but every man had their eye on you.'

'Not every man,' she said, fidgeting with her gloves.

He reached into his coat pocket and pulled out a small card. The diagonal corners propped between his fingers, it flickered between her own writing and an image of the Union Viaduct arched over a road. The *carte postale* she had sent him a few years ago. He had kept it.

'I won't lie, some days I couldn't bear to look at this. I felt bitter. Jealous. You were out there grabbing hold of the world, doing all the things we dreamt about, still the wild girl of Honeysuckle Street. While I stayed stuck in a crumbling house full of ghosts and with a man who hated me because I wasn't one.'

He tucked the card back into his inner coat pocket, next to his chest. Leaning across the carriage, he took hold of her hands. Iris kept her fingers bunched into fists against his broad palm. He stroked his thumb over her wrist, teasing at the buttons on her gloves, until, her skin humming, she capitulated. When she raised ramparts, he broke her not by battering, but with soft words and coercion. It had always been so between them, and while she wanted to resist and stay angry, the surrender felt familiar, and she almost enjoyed succumbing to his will. Her fury eased, her fists slackened, and she relaxed as her hand nestled against his. Pressing his thumb into her palm, he squeezed her fingers lightly, while she gripped him back.

'Iris, I'm here now. I know that doesn't make up for the past, but I could use a friend. And I think you could too.'

Iris thought to object. She had many friends. But then, none were quite like Hamish. None of them shared what they had. After all this time, friendship with Hamish was better than no Hamish at all.

'Hamish?' Iris said.

He squeezed her hand.

'Whatever the reason. I'm so glad you came home.'

CHAPTER SEVEN

The invitation had been a ridiculous idea. Ridiculous. Lord La-di-dah would have better offers by now, to proper parties and grand events. Not to tennis fundraisers on the neighbour's lawn, no matter how distinguished the neighbour.

'I do wish his grace had agreed to attend.' Iris's neighbour, Elise Hartright, flicked a blue and white check tablecloth into the air and guided it onto the wooden trestle. 'We could have charged double for tickets.'

Elise lived with her aged aunt in one of the modern townhouses on the opposite side of Honeysuckle Street, almost directly across from Hamish. The charity afternoon to raise funds for the women's hospital had been her idea, and like all her passions, Elise had thrown herself into the project with gusto. She had even convinced their neighbour the Duke of Osborne to allow them to host it on his ample lawn. The duke, appreciating that his address would boost interest in such an event, had agreed on two conditions: that the garden be returned to its exact state, and that no one expect him to attend.

'His grace would have been an attraction until they found him as sour as week old milk, and then everyone who had turned out a daughter in the hopes of making her a duchess would demand a refund. It is far better he is occupying himself elsewhere,' said Iris.

'Although you have invited a surprise earl, and an eligible one to boot. All those snobs who declined will regret their decision when they hear. I suppose I should practise my curtsy.'

'Don't you dare curtsy; it's only Hamish. And he isn't an earl, only an heir. And he won't come. He'll have better things to do.'

'Only Hamish?' came the deep voice behind her. Drat it. He always was a sneak. 'And what could be better than drinking lemonade and swinging a racquet on Duke Grumblepants's lawn?'

Iris swatted him with her cloth. 'Stop sneaking up on me.'

It had been a week since the trip to the theatre. Iris had seen Hamish only once in that time, from across the lawn at the Tatton's garden party, where he'd given her a polite wave before he returned his attention to his mallet, and his croquet partner, the younger Lady Miranda Tatton. Iris had left soon after, claiming fatigue before returning to her study and her preparations for her presentation to the board.

Iris introduced Hamish to Elise, and Elise, wanting to curtsy but also not wanting to, gave him an awkward sort of bow and a nervous giggle. Hamish smiled, swept up Elise's gloved hand, and with a tone that was incredibly sincere said, 'It's a pleasure to meet you, Miss Hartright.'

Elise remained motionless, then giggled again.

'Elise,' Iris said, nudging her friend. 'The first of your guests are arriving.'

By the gate, a small line of ladies had formed, all with racquets propped by their sides and tickets in their hands. Elise gave a small squeak and raced off.

'And you—' Iris turned and flicked him again with the cloth. 'When did you become so charming.'

'Steady on. Would you rather I carried on like a lout? Perhaps I shall just stand here all morning, eating biscuits and not smile at anyone.' Hamish said the word *biscuits* as Iris pulled a plate of them from one of the lined boxes they had carted over earlier. He snatched one up and took a bite. 'If you must know,' he continued, waving the half-eaten shortbread in his hand. 'Father had me take deportment lessons. It's nice to put them to use on delightful young ladies instead of his crusty old friends.'

Iris laid the plate on the table before retrieving a sponge cake from a basket and setting it down.

'You have become something of a marvel, haven't you?' Hamish looked up and down the table.

'Setting a table is not a challenge. You just lift things with your hands and place them.' She pulled a corked flask of lemonade from the basket and set it with a flourish. 'See?'

'Hilarious,' he said, then took another bite. 'Not only this. I mean all of your accomplishments. World traveller. Fundraiser. *Businesswoman*,' he added in a hush. 'And caring for your father. You really are a goddess. Do you have supernatural abilities I should be worried about?'

'I wish. I am afraid it's just me, although today is Elise's work. I am only here to help with the table.' She couldn't help but smile, her heart flushing with pride. So much of her work went unnoticed, or had to be hidden, and even a little praise made her glow.

'When do you sleep?' he continued, his voice still tinged with awe. 'And when do you have fun?'

'Fun?' Iris frowned. 'I have fun. I am having fun right now.'

He gave an exaggerated eye roll. 'Proper fun. Like what we used to have. Surely the wild girl of Honeysuckle Street can still cause mischief?'

She closed the lid on the hamper with a snap. 'The wild girl grew up a long time ago, I'm afraid. It's just boring old me and my numbers now.'

Hamish leaned over the table. 'I don't believe it. The wild girl's still in there. I'll coax her out,' he whispered, then straightened and spun his tennis racquet in the air. 'So, who is my prey?'

'I think you may have misunderstood. This isn't a competition, it's—'

Before Iris could explain the nature of the day, her eye was drawn to the gate where Gena, her skirts bunched in one hand, jittered like a dragonfly as she waited for a small group of ladies to file into the gardens. She skittered past the fence, then made a direct line for Iris.

'Miss Abberton. Oh, my heavens, Miss Abberton. Something terrible has happened.'

'I knew I shouldn't have left Papa.' Iris dropped the towel and stepped out from behind table, readying herself to run back to Number 4.

'Papa? Oh, your father is in the sitting room looking at his trophies, all is well with him. It's Mason. He's done himself an injury while helping me with some chores in the kitchen.'

Iris raised her brow. 'Mason? Helping with chores?'

Gena gave a huff. 'Well, not chores exactly. We were in the kitchen reciting our favourite soliloquies when he realised the time. He took the stairs at a run, slipped, and twisted his ankle.'

'Oh dear,' Iris said, her heart fluttering erratically with the rushing combination of relief and worry. 'Is he well?'

'Oh yes. Cook found him some tonic,' Gena said with a wave of her hand.

'Sherry?' Iris asked.

'She prefers to call it tonic. But his ankle is as thick as a tree trunk. He can't walk. I'm afraid he won't be able to run the demonstration.'

'Mason was going to give a tennis demonstration?' Hamish asked, his tone sceptical.

'He learnt a version of the game when he was in France touring with a circus troupe. Heavens, what shall we do?' Iris looked across to Elise, by the gate, still collecting tickets and chatting to the ladies.

'They can have a friendly game,' Hamish said as he lightly swung his racquet through the air. 'And one bite of these biscuits, they won't be bothered with tennis anyway.' As if to prove his point, Hamish grabbed a *petits fours* from the plate and took a bite, chewing enthusiastically and giving a soft sigh of appreciation. 'What demonstration? Problem solved.'

'Except,' Iris dropped her voice. 'None of them know how to play.'

'You organised a tennis tournament where no one knows how to play?' Hamish asked.

'No, Elise organised a fundraiser to *demonstrate* how to play. And afterwards, any enthusiastic ladies could have a casual whack between themselves.'

'A casual whack? Have you ever seen ladies play tennis? There's nothing casual about it,' he said, incredulous.

'I'm sorry Lord La-Di-Dah, but not every miss has a swathe of private instructors at her disposal, and many are too scared to try at a club in case they make a fool of themselves. Elise thought that a less formal event might encourage some of them to try and decide for themselves if they would like to take their interest further.'

The half-smile on Hamish's lips froze under the rampage of her outburst. A more modest lady would have apologised, but Iris was not in the mood to be that sort of lady.

'I'll go tell them,' Iris said, dropping her cloth to the table. The ladies were standing in small, nervous groups. Elise, by the gate, looked across with a puzzled frown. Iris's heart tore. Her friend would be devastated.

'I will teach them.' Hamish announced, slightly regally, like he was volunteering to take a message behind enemy lines.

'Please don't tease, Hamish,' Iris said, exasperated.

'I will have you know...' He unbuttoned his coat, shrugged it off, and laid it over the edge of the table. 'A tournament between neighbouring estates was the highlight of my summers at Caplin House. I am reigning champion, three years running.' He turned towards the assembled groups. 'Ladies. Slight change of plans. I will be your instructor.'

Iris didn't know the collective noun for a group of ladies swooning, or even if there was such a term, but if there was, she would have used it to describe the transformation that swept over those gathered on the Duke of Osborne's lawn. Hamish stepped out of the shade of the marquee, his dark hair lustrous under the late winter sunshine, his biceps flexing beneath his shirt sleeves. He turned and gave her a wink, his familiar dimples kissing each cheek, before he strode before the hastily hung net and faced the assembly.

Elise ushered the last attendee over, then joined Iris beneath the marquee. 'Your earl is going to teach? Forget the duke. Next time, we'll arrange Lord Dalton. And charge triple!'

Iris helped Elise lay the spread, and when finished, Elise took up her new racquet and snuck to the back of the group. Iris had played the game a few times when travelling but found it not to her taste—she preferred less competitive exercise, like walking or a good country ramble. The type of activity that allowed her to meet with people, take in the countryside, and if she was lucky, feel the heartbeat of a place. She untied her apron and placed it beside Hamish's coat, then spread out a blanket on the grass and sat, grateful for a chance to rest.

The ladies had all relaxed enough that they threw light, encouraging remarks to one another in between gaps in Hamish's instructions. First, he gave a brief overview of the rules, and then, demonstrated the basic swings. Hidden by the shadow and the brim of her hat, Iris found her eyes trailing over the stretch of his muscles as he moved. His lankiness had evolved into litheness, and with each swing, his taut form stretched against the fine shirt linen. She'd gingerly cherished the memory of Hamish and her making love, like it was a fragile ornament, and after he left, had managed to separate it from her sadness and anger. Since that night, so much about him had changed. He was stronger now. Taller too, and more self-assured. Would he feel the same as he pressed his weight against her? Would his body still fit against her curves? Would he still kiss her with exploratory curiosity? Would Hamish the man be able to rouse her the same? Would he bother to try, or take his fill and discard her?

He removed his hat, spun it across the lawn, then wiped his hand across his forehead. Lady Miranda, closest to Iris, sighed. Jealousy nibbled her stomach, and she pushed the feeling down. It was pointless to ruminate on what could never be.

'Thank you, ladies. That should give you the basics. Perhaps you would like to try...' Hamish shot her a quick glance and winked. 'A casual whack amongst yourselves?' He sauntered back, stopping occasionally to answer a question or to demonstrate a swing, obviously enjoying the attention. He paused by the table, poured two glasses of lemonade, and handed one to Iris before he sat down beside her on the rug.

Iris sipped her lemonade, grateful for the coolness to quench the heat inside. He took a long draught, half emptying his glass, then leaned back on his elbows.

'I think every woman here is besotted with you. You could take your pick of a bride right now,' she said.

'Go on then.' He nudged his foot against hers. 'Help me choose. But no one lower than a viscount's daughter.'

'My, Lord La-di-dah, you have become a proper toff, haven't you?' Iris spoke low, but clear. Hamish had never been hung up on titles when they were young.

He chuckled, although his laughter held a bitter tinge. 'Father's orders, not my wishes. What about those two, tapping a ball between the net. Who are they?'

Iris tucked her knees up and sat forward a little. 'Miss Robertson and Miss Wallace. Both daughters of barons, so too lowly for you. And the lovely Miss Wade over there—' she took a sharp intake of breath, miming shock. 'Is the child of a mere merchant. Her father is desperate to have her join the *ton*. Along with being a beauty and a skilled musician, her allowance is some £200 a year, and her dowry could not only repair Caplin House but rebuild it. Twice.'

'But still a commoner? Father wouldn't stand it.'

'Your father would not make an exception for a ludicrous amount of money?' she asked, knowing he would.

'My orders are clear. Who else?'

'Lady Felicity Archer is second daughter of a marquess, although one with empty coffers. Her sister married Huxley Pemberton, presumptive heir to a viscount. Although she is determined to marry for love, like her sister.'

'Love? Love has no place in marriage. Only makes things messy.' Hamish popped a small square of seed cake into his mouth and chewed thoughtfully. 'That excellent advice came from my mother, who certainly knew what a marriage without love was.'

'That leaves the vibrant Miss Hilary, who will guarantee you a loveless marriage, as the rumour is she prefers the company of her lady's maid.'

'Would I be allowed to watch?' he asked.

'I think not.'

'Next!'

'And finally, we come to Lady Miranda Tatton, the lovely girl you already met at her mother's garden party. And *she* has barely taken her eyes from you all afternoon.' Iris's voice stretched as she spoke, and while she determined to keep her focus on the grass, she couldn't help but let her eyes flick to Hamish. He watched Lady Miranda intently as she swung her racquet a few times before tossing the ball into the air, swinging, and narrowly missing it. The ball fell to the ground with a dull thump before rolling a few feet away, and Lady Miranda giggled as she chased it, before scooping it up to try again. Even failing at something, she was lovely. The right class. A healthy dowry. Iris could almost hear the church bells chiming.

'Did you see her serve? I could never be married to a woman who serves so badly.'

'A serve in tennis is only a minor thing,' Iris said.

'Tennis is the only enjoyable activity at Caplin House. Father does not have the stamina to walk out to the court and his voice does not carry that far. My one pleasure would be ruined by a woman with a weak wrist.'

'You have dismissed every eligible young lady here. Do you know what I think Lord La-di-dah? I think you don't really want to get married.'

'There is one woman you missed,' he said, a smirk tugging at the corner of his mouth.

'Elise? I am not letting you even consider courting my dear neighbour. She has been through enough.'

'Not Elise. I meant you.' Mischief danced in his eyes.

'Me?' Her mouth went dry. 'The problem there is obvious.' *Bastard child of a whore. Adopted from the streets. Trumped up daughter of a trader. Blood will out.* The insults Hamish's father had hurled at her, just two days before the accident, at the meeting she had never told anyone about, not even Hamish, rang in her ears. Iris swallowed the sting of them, then lifted her chin and met his eyes. 'You see, Lord La-di-dah, you said it yourself. I am Iris, daughter of the goddess Diana, and a goddess myself. *You* are a mere mortal. I believe that makes me out of your league.'

His lips twitched, before he threw back his head and laughed, a deep, hearty laugh, the sort reserved for friends who knew each other very well but could still surprise one another. It landed on her skin and made it tingle. A few ladies nearby turned. Mrs Crofts, their neighbour who had a way of sniffing out rumours, lifted a fan across her face and leaned closer to her friend. Iris waved them away. To hear Hamish laugh openly and without burden had been worth any gossip they might conjure.

'So, tell me,' Hamish said as he leaned back on his elbows and looked across the lawn. 'Which country has the best lovers?'

'Best lovers? I'm not sure I like what you're implying.'

'No judgement, I'm only curious. Iris Abberton, world explorer, the wild girl of Honeysuckle Street, surely has a lover on every continent. Meanwhile, I've been amusing bored country wives and the occasional tavern wench.' He met her eyes briefly, then looked to his boots. 'So, tell me, who is it. The French? Italians?'

That errant curl had fallen over his forehead again, and Iris resisted the impulse to lean forward and push it back. Which lovers, he had asked. What to say?

'Englishmen,' she said as she tucked her hands in to her lap. He raised a curious eyebrow. 'They make love like they have something to prove.'

Chapter Eight

The second hand pivoted in a steady circumference, and as it passed the XII again, the minute hand lumbered forward. Hamish snapped the plate closed and stuffed his pocket watch back into his coat. Forty minutes. Forty minutes he had been kept waiting in the entrance, even though his aunt had specified eleven sharp.

His agitation gnawed this morning. He'd laid in bed upon waking, clinging to his dreamscape as the morning sun crept across his pillow. He barely dreamt at Caplin House. The place didn't allow any frivolity or escape, even in the privacy of one's sleep.

But last night, he had dreamt of Iris and their first time, both hers and his. The two of them fumbling in the dark, not knowing what to do but somehow also knowing exactly what to do, guided by each other's hands, each other's mouth, and each other's moans. The memory had not just returned but had crashed into his consciousness with explicit clarity, and when the last relics of sweetness had slipped away, he'd remained buried in the blankets. He could almost smell the gentle wave of lavender and spice off her skin, mingled with sweat and want. Women's smiles were meant to hide their secrets, but he knew hers, and rather than quell his fascination, it only stoked his hunger. And damn himself if all he could think of was whether she still tasted as sweet.

He pulled out his pocket watch. Seven minutes to midday.

'For heaven's sake, Aunt Tilly, this is ridiculous.'

Hamish was about to call into the hallway for the butler who had admitted him, when the unmistakable sound of his aunt's high laughter flittered down from the floor above.

'What the devil?' he muttered. But it came again, louder and clearer, and before Hamish could question his manners, he took the stairs two at a time, past the ugly Greek ewer, until he stood at the entrance to his aunt's sitting room, where he found her seated at the table with a man in a dark suit with slicked back hair, Between them sat a bottle of champagne and two half-depleted glasses.

'Hamish darling,' his aunt called as she extended her hand in affectionate welcome. 'So lovely of you to join us.'

'Lovely? I've been waiting downstairs for the best part of an hour!'

'And there, my boy,' said the man in the chair. 'Is your first lesson. A rake does not arrive on time. And he certainly does not wait for an invitation to join a party.' He turned to face Hamish. 'Algernon Pascoe. Pleased to make your acquaintance.'

'It's you. It's bloody you, from the club.' Hamish stomped across the room. 'I received your bill, thank you very much. I thought you would have one drink, not half a bottle.'

'Lesson number three. Take what life offers, then find a way to take a little more.' Algernon chuckled and gave his thin moustache a twist. 'Your aunt has of course told me about you, but let's have a look.'

Algernon walked around Hamish. Hamish swivelled to keep his eye on him, until Algernon grabbed his shoulders, and with a short bark, ordered, 'Stay!' He completed his circumference, then came to stand beside Aunt Tilly.

'Much work is needed. But there is plenty of potential. I agree.'

'Agree? To what?' Hamish asked.

'To rake lessons, of course. Isn't that what you wanted?' Aunt Tilly said.

Hamish looked from Algernon to his aunt. 'I wanted introductions. Invitations. I don't need *lessons*. I can be quite the cad at times.'

'Bedding your neighbour's bored wife does not make you a rake.' Algernon spoke with a nonchalant air, not even looking up from his examination of his fingernails. 'Although it does bode well for your potential. Now, first things first. This suit...'

Hamish gave his aunt a questioning glare, which she replied to with a shrug and a smile before reaching for her champagne flute and taking a sip. Algernon snapped his fingers twice. From the corner of the room, a small man with gold-rimmed spectacles, grey and black flecked hair, and a tape measure around his neck emerged and scurried to Algernon's side.

'What do you make of this, Quigley?' Algernon gestured loosely at Hamish.

'And who the devil are you?' Hamish asked, looking about. Was anyone else squirrelled away in his aunt's sitting room?

'Clifton Quigley. Tailor.' He didn't offer his hand, only put a finger to the side of his cheek and pouted in thought.

'I am not looking for a tailor,' Hamish tried to explain. 'My father has sent all my measurements to Drakeford and Sons.'

Quigley gave a huff. 'And it shows. Black on black? How did you imagine such an amazing combination?' Quigley slipped the tape from around his neck and flicked it around Hamish's chest, then down his torso, and lastly across his shoulders. He pulled his scissors from his belt, and before Hamish could register what was happening, Quigley slid the blade beneath his waistcoat buttons and snipped. They popped free and Quigley caught them— *one, two, three, four*.

'Steady on!' Hamish batted Quigley away with one hand and pulled his coat closed with the other.

'The buttons are good. The rest... I lack words.' He turned away as if the sight of the black waistcoat tortured him. 'Ready in time for this evening?'

'Correct.' Algernon replied.

Quigley took out his watch, gave a nod, then tucked it away. 'I'll have the boy deliver it by seven o'clock.' He gave Hamish a nod. 'A pleasure, my lord. I look forward to addressing the rest of this' He waved his hand in the air in some vague indication of Hamish's outfit. 'Have a pleasant evening.'

The clock in the hall struck noon, and Hamish, whirling from the sudden lurch between boredom and extreme activity, lowered himself into one of the chairs to take stock.

'Refreshment?' His aunt pushed a flute, half full of sparkling champagne, across the table.

Hamish grabbed the glass and took a swig.

'Typical of Algernon, you have already met,' she said, looking at her friend. 'He knows every green lord better than he knows which pub waters down their ale, or which gent is spending more time with a new mistress instead of his wife. He is a cad, a scoundrel, and a wastrel, frequently in debt—'

'But never in debtors' prison.' Algernon sat down at the table with them and took up his glass. 'I'm very proud of that fact.'

'Only because you have gullible friends who bail you out.' Aunt Tilly and Algernon exchanged a look. It wasn't hard to deduce who had paid a share of the bills. 'But despite—or perhaps because of—all these failings, Algernon is one of my oldest friends. He is a committed rake. He will teach you everything you need to know.'

'I told you,' Hamish protested. 'I don't need lessons. All I need is some introductions—'

'Hamish. May I, my lord, call you Hamish?' Algernon asked.

Hamish gave a nod. 'You may.'

'When you were learning to ride, did you meet the stable master, do a lap of the yards on a pony, and then declare yourself competent?'

'Well, no—'

'And when you hunt pheasant, do you just stomp out onto the moors and start shooting at anything that twitches?'

'Actually, I don't hunt, but my brother used too—'

Algernon leaned forward and spoke in a mock whisper. 'And when you set your eye on one of your country misses, do you make a house call, declare your intentions, and expect an invitation to the boudoir?'

'Sometimes it takes weeks.' Hamish couldn't help but mimic the man's smile. 'The chase is almost as fun as the victory.'

'Of course, it is.' Algernon gave him a knowing wink. 'If you have come to London to have a few wild nights, lose some coin at the races, and risk the health of your bollocks at the docks, then I will give you a list of names, fun lords who will help you. But if you mean to do some serious damage to your family name, it will take time.' Algernon fixed him with a knowing look. Aunt Tilly had clearly already informed Algernon of his vendetta against his father. 'You will need to be known. Invited in, but all the while creating mischief in the shadows. And then—only then—do you shock them with a right proper scandal.'

'Of course. Otherwise, I'm just another naughty heir. And father would call me home at the first hint of disobedience. It's brilliant.' Excitement bubbled in Hamish's chest. For the first time in many years, he felt like he was in charge of his own life.

Aunt Tilly rolled her eyes. 'I wouldn't say *brilliant*.'

'You can't do this half-hearted, my boy. All in, so they say. Are you committed?'

'Yes. I'm committed. I'll attend every event and play the part of a proper young lord.'

Algernon nodded, almost as enthusiastic as Hamish. 'But first, if you want to become a rake, you must understand what it is to *be* a rake. You must appreciate the legacy you are dedicating yourself to.'

Aunt Tilly gave a small groan. 'Really, Algernon? Must we have the history of rakes?'

'My dear, ours is a fine pedigree. We are more than just naughty boys. If young Hamish here is to succeed, he must appreciate that heritage. Now...' Algernon stood, took a quick swig, and began to pace. 'It all officially began back in 1718, when Philip, Duke of Wharton, founded the first Hellfire Club, right here in London...'

Aunt Tilly turned to her butler, made a movement with her hands, and then turned back to Hamish. When the butler reappeared, he set two goblets on the table, uncorked a bottle, and glugged claret into the glasses. Tilly pushed one across the table for Hamish and pulled the second one towards herself.

'When he says "hell," you take a sip. When he says "rake," I'll take a sip. And when he says "sandwich," we both drain our goblets. Understand?'

'Shouldn't I be paying attention?' Hamish whispered to Aunt Tilly, his ear still tilted towards Algernon in case he missed something important.

'Algernon's commitment to rakery is admirable, but it can be a little overzealous. You will hear these stories again, trust me,' she said.

'No one can be sure exactly *when* the term rake was first used... ' Algernon continued, unperturbed.

Aunt Tilly picked up her glass and took a sip.

'But it is believed that the term was in use by the mid-1700s, when a club, ostensibly called Hellfire or Hell-rake...'

Aunt Tilly gave a nod towards Hamish's untouched glass. 'It's a two-hour lecture.'

'Two hours?' Hamish picked up his glass and took a sip. Warm and sweet claret. Delicious. 'But why sandwich?'

'It was the fourth Earl of Sandwich...'

Aunt Tilly gave him a wink. 'Bottoms up, my dear.'

CHAPTER NINE

'I've been roaming! I've been roaming!
  Where the honeysuckle creeps—'

The knocker thumped against the front door again, a dull clap resounding through the house. Iris trotted down the stairs, her slippers patting against the wood. She arrived in the foyer almost at the same time as Mason.

'I thought I heard... Iris said, just as Mason opened the door to reveal Hamish propped against the door frame. 'Hamish! What on earth are you doing here?'

'And like a bee I'm coming.' As Hamish sang, he swung through the door, flinging his arms wide. His boots splattered mud onto the rug. Mason hummed a few notes, then burst into song in accompaniment.

'With its kisses on my lips!'

Then they both laughed, and Mason shut the door behind Hamish.

'Thank you, Mason. If the entire street weren't aware that Lord Dalton is inebriated, they are now,' Iris said.

Mason gave an embarrassed nod. 'Sorry, miss.' Then he nudged Hamish. 'Fabulous voice, my lord.'

'Heavens.' Iris put a gloved hand under her nose. 'Did you fall into a brewer's vat? You reek.'

Coat unbuttoned, with damp trouser cuffs and wearing the most hideous waistcoat in all of England, Hamish fell back against the door with a giggle. He looked down at a blue and white multi-spouted jug that dangled from his hand.

'I've been drinking from this puzzle jug. Just here.' He jerked it to eye level, and Iris cringed as a little ale sloshed over the edge and dripped onto the floor. 'To drink from the puzzle jug, one must figure out its secret. If you guess right, you get to have a drink.' He pressed a finger against a series of holes along the side of the jug, covering some and exposing others, mumbling, 'This one? No, this one,' to himself before he tipped it back. Amber ale gushed from one of the spouts and splashed against his face. 'Oops.' He smiled, licking the drips from his lips. 'Wrong one.'

'I know what a puzzle jug is, we import them from Norway. Why do you have one, and why are you here? Did you miss your house?'

'Spies, Iris.' He flung a hand in the general direction of Number 8. 'The lot of them. If I go home, they'll tell my father I was drinking. And they can't tell my father, not yet. That would spoil the surprise.' He giggled again, and twisting the jug thoughtfully to try another spout, he tilted it, this time with more success. Hamish then looked from the jug to Iris, then back again, before he thrust it out in front of him. 'Where's my manners. D'youse want some?'

'I think you've had enough for the both of us.' She levered the jug from his hand and set it down on the sideboard. 'Mason, help me keep Lord Dalton steady. Between us we can help him into the parlour.'

'But Gena says the parlour is only for special occasions,' Mason said as he darted around to Hamish's opposite side.

'I would say a soused lord is a special occasion, wouldn't you? This way, and then please fetch a bucket, in case his lordship decides to turn our rug the same horrendous shade as his waistcoat.'

'You don't like my waistcoat?' Hamish slurred as he leaned heavily into Iris and took a staggered step forward. 'I thought it looked dapper.'

'Why don't you ask Spencer about your waistcoat.' The grey tom had found his way into the parlour and lay stretched out on the chaise. He rolled, exposing his belly as he pawed playfully at the air. 'This morning, he brought up a hairball a similar shade. Maybe he will like it.'

'Spencer likes my waistcoat,' Hamish said with a dreamy smile and a hiccough. 'Do you think Father would like it?'

Iris laughed. 'He most definitely would not.'

Hamish sniggered. 'Good. I pick my own tailor now. I'm not a child.'

They had reached the lounge, and with Mason's help, she lowered Hamish onto the cushion. Hamish groaned, and Mason left to search for a bucket. Iris grabbed a pillow from a nearby chair and stuffed it into the corner. She pushed against Hamish's arm. For a moment he resisted, the muscles beneath his shirt bunching. 'Hamish, you cannot go home,' she said softly. 'You need to rest.'

He gave a yawn, then relaxed and fell onto his side. Iris pulled her favourite blanket from a nearby storage box.

'This blanket,' she said as she shook it out over him. 'Was made with wool that was a gift from a merchant in Sydney. The softest you've ever felt, and my favourite. So please—please—be careful with it.'

The delicate knit fell over him, following the awkward angles of his body until it covered him from his neck to his knees. As Iris tucked it closer around his shoulders, he snuggled and gathered it under his chin before his eyes closed. Iris perched on the footstool beside him. His expression mellowed as he began to doze, and his breathing dropped into a steady rhythm. The tight lines around his mouth relaxed, then disappeared into his soft, full cheeks, and the worried creases along his forehead smoothed.

Curled up on his side with his lashes flickering, he seemed torn in time, stuck between the petulant man he seemed intent on becoming and the boy still hoping for the smallest bit of attention. His face tightened, and he mumbled into a dream. Not a nice one, perhaps. She caressed his cheek, hot and flushed, and ran her thumb over his brow until his jaw slackened. His lips, the same shade of pink she remembered, parted slightly, and she trailed a finger across their plumpness, recalling only too vividly the tenderness of them, and how they made her heart ache.

A cough broke the quiet, and Iris pushed herself back and scrambled to her feet. Heavens, had anyone seen her? The staff were unlikely to spread rumours through town, but they did like to gossip, and gossip could always be overheard.

Iris let out a slow breath of relief. 'I didn't hear the door. Good morning, Jonah.'

Once a week, Jonah Worthington called to see her father. One of his oldest friends, Jonah had aged into a refined, artistic, silver-haired man, while Papa had seemed to age grey. A successful painter who lived in Soho amongst the aesthetic crowd, Jonah was the reason her house was staffed by a cast of failed performers. She sometimes imagined him walking the streets looking for artists and actors who had heard one rejection too many. She did her best to accommodate them, just like Papa had always done. Some she was able to set up in the factory. Others, younger and more adventurous, occasionally found work on a ship. Papa never refused Jonah's requests, and now, she was unable to refuse him either. After all, she owed him so much.

'Entertaining this morning?' he asked, eyebrows raised. He took a few steps into the room and peered over the lounge before giving her a smirk. 'Dalton. Interesting.'

'Papa is in the sitting room upstairs,' she said, not quite meeting his eye. 'I'll show you in.'

Iris held her skirts clear of her feet as she traipsed up the stairs, half daring Jonah to make some remark, but half dreading it too. Apprehensive with waiting, she turned, intending to goad him into just saying what he was thinking, when she saw the pensive lines across his brow and the set determination of his jaw. Chiding herself for her arrogance, she instead focused on her slippers. So much could change in a week with Papa, so much depended on what type of day he was having. And for Jonah, who didn't dare visit more often, the change could sometimes be shocking. He hid the toll it took so well.

Once inside the sitting room, Iris closed the door and softly turned the lock as Jonah, hat grasped in his hand, took the seat opposite Papa. He didn't speak. Just lowered himself and waited to be noticed. After a time, Papa looked across at the man who had been his companion for more than half his life. The man who had come travelling with them, who had painted the map on her wall, who had been a firm if discreet fixture of birthdays and celebrations. The man Papa loved, and who loved him. Iris forced herself to breathe as she waited, hoping, desperately praying for Papa to remember Jonah.

Papa stared for a long time. Recognition flittered between short spasms of confusion and frustration before his eyes softened a little and he reached out his hand. 'Jonah,' he said, his voice warm. 'How kind of you to visit.'

Relief flooded Jonah's face, his smile a warm beam. He took Papa's hand and leaned forward to press his lips against it, then sat back, his thumb absent-mindedly stroking. They'd lived their lives like this. Small moments captured in secrecy. Tenderness snatched in quiet moments. Not hiding for fear of gossip, but real fear for their lives and their freedom.

Iris slipped through the interconnecting door into her study and took up her seat at the desk. Watching Jonah and Papa tore at her heart most days, and today the agony seared. She grieved for Jonah, who might one day sit in that chair and not be recognised, and today it felt like that day loomed incredibly close. And for Papa, who clutched at memories like they were dust motes, always swirling out of reach. And, in a moment of selfishness, she felt sad for herself.

How she wanted what they had. Not the secrecy or the loss, but the light of their days that they had shared before now. The tenderness. The belonging. The way they caught one another's eye in a room and shared a small smile of connection. How on long train trips they would lean into one another without realising, occupying each other's space with casual intimacy.

But never would she have that. Because no matter how well-suited they were, or how advantageous the match would be, she knew she would never look at any man the way Jonah looked at Papa. She would never be in thrall of his presence or smile just because he had entered a room. Because for as long as her days had light in them, for as long as she'd raced through streets and clambered up trees in a grubby dress, for as far back as her memory reached, she had been in love with the awkward and lanky son of an earl two doors over.

Even as a forgotten second son he had been out of reach. And now? He may have been drunkenly sprawled on the lounge in her parlour, but he could have been on the moon. Not only for his father's order to find a bride no lower than a viscount's daughter, but because he saw her as he'd always seen her. As the scrappy girl next door. As a friend.

Iris threw the pen onto the desk, then cursed herself as a thin line of ink splattered over the wood. She rummaged through the stacks of cards and notes to find a slip of blotting paper, then laid it lightly over the spatter and watched the paper darken as it absorbed the spill.

Jonah tapped at the door before entering. He set his own tea on the desk before placing another cup before her, then sunk into Papa's chair. 'Albert's asleep.' He twisted his cup on the saucer. 'He's declining.'

'Today just isn't a good day,' she said, not wanting to meet the pain in Jonah's eyes, but forcing herself to look up. 'Just last week, he looked at a folder and he remembered, I know he did. And—'

Jonah held up his hand to silence her as his expression curled with anguish. 'Have you spoken with the doctor?'

'You want him strapped in a straitjacket and carted off to Bedlam? No, I have not consulted the doctor. He's losing his memory, not his mind.' She spoke with more venom than Jonah deserved, but the suggestion rankled. The doctor had ceased being useful months before.

Jonah held up his hands in defence. 'Jesus, Iris, of course that's not what I want.' He took in the stacks of books and papers before him, all of them facing her way when once they would have been spread evenly between the seats. 'But seeing you like this, working yourself senseless, hiding behind a shell of engagements and fundraisers all while caring for him, it's not what he wanted for you. You can't continue like this. You'll exhaust yourself.'

Jonah gave her a strained smile and sipped his tea. Iris picked up her own cup and wrapped her hands around the warm porcelain. The faint snores from Papa rumbled along as a background to the silence between them. Not awkward, but not companionable either. The last few years had taken a toll, and on days like today, her connection with Jonah frayed. It was with a bitterness she watched him, knowing he could leave and go back to his artistic life, but also with a pained gratitude because she knew that they had chosen to live their lives apart so that her father could grow Abberton and Co and raise his adopted daughter with the veneer of respectability.

'Dalton found you.' Jonah flicked her a look at her that suggested he knew more than he was letting on.

'He didn't want to go home in his state. He says the staff will tell his father,' she added as a weak explanation.

'He made a cake of himself in Haymarket last night.' Jonah huffed a small laugh. Nothing in this town slipped by him. 'After he solved the mystery of the puzzle jug and shouted a few rounds of rum, he said he wanted to learn how to sing like a sailor. He wandered the docks, begging for someone to teach him sea shanties. The sailors were not impressed, as they had moved on to *other* activities by then. One of them cuffed him, and Algernon Pascoe of all people got him into a hackney to send him home.'

'Pascoe? Never heard of him,' she said.

'He's a cad and a mooch. Used to be spectacular but now is a bit shabby and derelict. Spends his time with the discarded mistresses of lords, the ones who were astute enough to save a few coins anyway.'

Iris snorted at the ridiculous image of Hamish, in his hideous outfit, trying to learn bawdy tunes. Jonah didn't smile with her though, just watched her over his tea before setting the cup down with a clink.

'Be careful, Iris,' he said.

'Are you warning me away from him?'

'I would never do such a thing, you're a grown woman. I'm only concerned. You are strong, but you are not made for scandal.'

'He's just lost. His father kept him cooped up on the estate all this time, and he's enjoying the freedom by letting off steam. Once he adjusts to society, starts courting some fine young lady, he'll settle. Probably take a villa in Mayfair and set up a mistress in the house.' The thought bit. Hopefully Spencer would scratch her.

'I've seen men like Hamish before.' Jonah spoke with a knowing tone. 'Men lost in torture and grief. A few make it their genius, but most lose themselves in drink and self-pity instead of facing their demons.'

'Hamish is not a tortured artist,' she said.

Jonah took his hat from the desk. 'Lords just do it with more panache. Trust me, Iris, Lord Dalton means to go down. Don't get tangled up with him on his descent.'

CHAPTER TEN

The clock that hung over the mantle in the downstairs kitchen chimed the hour— *bong, bong, bong, bong*. Hamish splashed water onto his face, scooped a handful into his mouth, and swished before spitting into the basin. Eyes closed, he grasped until his hand brushed against the towel that Gena had left for him, dabbing the soft cotton over his forehead.

Take what life offers, then find a way to take a little more.

Algernon's lesson rang in Hamish's ears. He hadn't arrived on the Abberton doorstep with the intention of encroaching, but now he had done it, he raged between wanting to apologise and feeling elated that he had done something his father would disapprove of. Something *roguish*. The problem with the Abberton staff was that they seemed to find his sleeping in the front parlour all day amusing. Damn actors.

Tugging on his coat, Hamish stepped out of the laundry and walked down the short corridor into the kitchen. Gena was crouched before the stove, and as he walked by, she straightened and turned to deposit a tray of biscuits on the long wooden work bench.

'All sorted now, my lord?' she asked, her lips twitching.

'Ahh, yes. Thank you. I would have asked Miss Abberton to use the guest washroom, but I thought I should—'

'Stop smelling like the Thames in summer before you went to see her?'

'Something like that,' he said, grinning. 'Mind if I?' His fingers tickled the air, just over the tray. Shortbread. He hadn't eaten since breakfast the day before, and the crisp, sweet smell sent his stomach grumbling.

'Show some patience, if you can, and I'll bring up a plate.' Gena flicked him with a towel, and then her eyes turned wide with horror. Hamish took a sharp intake of breath, feigning shock. Gena's smile dissolved. 'Apologies, my lord. I quite forgot myself.'

A smile tugged his lips before a laugh burst out. 'For that, I'm taking one now.' He snatched a biscuit off the tray. 'And I may steal Iris's when you bring them up.'

Gena flicked him with the towel again. 'Still all cheek. Come on then, I'll show you up so you can beg your apologies. Miss Iris has been in her study all day. A break would do her good.'

Hamish followed Gena up the stairs, from the lower ground floor to the entry at street level, then rounded the banister to ascend to the first floor. She led him into the sitting room, then through the small side door that led to what had been Iris's playroom, but now seemed to be her study.

Iris, who sat at a wide partners desk, glanced up at him as he entered, then bent her head over her papers with a frown. She flicked through a stack, mumbling to herself before opening one folder, then another. After a moment she retrieved a sheet, set it on her ledger, took up her pen, and began to write, her gaze flicking between the note and the page.

'If I can just finish January,' she said as she plucked another sheet from the pile. 'Then you can grovel an apology for spreading mud through my parlour.'

She didn't look up as she spoke, only kept her eyes on the work before her. Every time she rummaged and pulled out a sheet, a victorious beam flashed across her delicate face, and the thin gold-wire spectacles perched on her nose emphasised her green eyes, which sparkled with each triumph like the sun glinting off water. He never felt enamoured when bent over the ledgers for Caplin House. The tally of rents, the harvest, and the expenses bored him. He managed them, but with a groan. Amid her numbers, Iris came alive.

'Care for some tea?' Gena asked as she slid the tray onto the desk and placed a cup and saucer before him, and then Iris. 'Although it is late in the afternoon. Perhaps you would like something stronger, my lord? Wine? Brandy?'

Hamish winced as his stomach churned. 'Tea would be fine.'

'I'll bring up biscuits,' Gena said with a wink. 'As soon as they have cooled.' She placed the teapot on the desk, then took the tray and walked towards the door.

'Gena, are you not staying?' Iris looked up from her work with slight alarm. 'To chaperone?'

Gena waved her hand. 'It's only Hamish. I mean, Lord Dalton. And it's not like you're a fresh chick anymore, is it? Many a woman dispenses with a chaperone once they reach thirty.'

'I am not thirty yet,' Iris huffed.

Gena waved her cloth as she left the room. 'You're the one for the numbers. I'll be just downstairs anyways. I shan't be long. Shout if Lord Hamish tries to seduce you.'

Hamish smothered a laugh as Iris stared after her housemistress in disbelief.

'While you complain of being treated like a child, every-one is keen to remind me how old I am. There must be less than three weeks between us.'

'Fifteen days, if I remember. But you don't look a day over twenty-eight.'

'Why thank you, Lord La-di-dah.' Iris said with a hefty dose of sarcasm, then leaned over her ledger again.

'Drat.' Hamish lifted his cup out of the way as Spencer launched himself onto his lap, narrowly saving the brew from spilling over. Spencer needled at Hamish's thighs before turning in a small circle, his paws pushing uncom-fortably into his legs until he curled himself into a tight, pudgy ball of grey and white fluff.

'So does shedding all over my waistcoat mean you like it?' He scratched Spencer under an ear. 'Or is this your way of improving it?'

Spencer narrowed his eyes until they closed, tucked his paws beneath him, and gave a low, rumbling purr.

'I'll take that as you like it.'

Iris stifled a laugh. 'He's gathering inspiration for his next furball, which he will hopefully deposit on your doorstep instead of mine.'

Hamish pulled the tea towards him and took a sip. Gena had remembered how he took it—sugar, no milk—and with that first, invigorating sip, he felt half alive again, like a withered and naked branch shedding its winters chill to sprout forth a supple spring shoot. He clicked his tongue, waiting for Iris to pay attention to him, but she remained absorbed in her work. He gave a little whistle. No response.

'Iris, Iris,' he half sang as he swivelled on the chair. 'Here I thought you were the wild one. You have become dull without me.'

The bait worked, although a little too well, as she looked up so fast it was like he had jabbed her with a poker, and when she spoke it wasn't with a quick, friendly retort, but with anger. 'We can't all spend our days buying ugly waistcoats. Some of us have obligations.'

'I have obligations—' he started, but she cut him off.

'January, Hamish. I must finish January.' And she leaned over her papers again.

She had always had a slight stubbornness to her, and he knew it would do no good to interrupt, so instead he amused himself in trying to remember how the room had looked when they were young, but very little remained. The bears, cats, rabbits, and all the playful motifs of childhood that Mr Abberton's friend—his *special* friend—Mr Worthington had painted were replaced by cedar wooden panelling that reached about four feet up the wall. The plaster had been tinted a soft cream, like the parlour, and with the fire crackling, the room felt like being encased in a comforting cup of chocolate or a hot coffee. On the far wall, in the artist hand he recognised, a world map stretched from floor to ceiling. It had been covered in notes, so that it appeared ruffled, like a cockerel with its feathers up and itching for excitement.

Spencer gave a small mew of protest as Hamish tucked his hand beneath his furry body and shifted him onto the chair, then he went to investigate the mural at the far end of the room. Now closer, he saw that the pinned notes were a jumble of photographs, *cartes postales*, tickets, and sketches. Mostly of Iris and her father, and the odd picture with Mr Worthington, but also pyramids, buildings, bridges, and factories. But he couldn't help but focus on the images of Iris on horseback, on a camel, and in a rickshaw. While he had been sequestered away in the country, Iris had seen the world. The places they dreamt of as children, had ogled over as illustrations in books, had become her memories. For him, they remained as dreams. Envy and regret curled through him and swirled into a familiar pool of resentment.

Hamish ran his finger along the edge of a line drawing pinned over Canada. He instantly recognised Iris seated somewhere, although not posing, but slumped against a window; eyes closed, her hair spilled over one shoulder and almost into her lap.

'Papa sketched that.' Iris's skirts brushed against his shin. 'I was so cross with him. I told him he should have woken me to tell me my hair had come lose, and that I was snoring in first class.' She drew a line across the map with her finger to the centre of the country. 'He wanted to ride the Grand Trunk Railway. He had the sketch in his pocket when all our bags were stolen at an outpost. We had to hop a train to get to Toronto.' She half laughed. 'He had already climbed in, but I couldn't keep up and I was still running. I thought I wasn't going to make it and would be left behind, but he leaned out and grabbed my wrist. I was running so fast, and he held on so tight, I thought I'd snap. When he finally hauled me up, I burst into tears. "I'd never leave you my darling girl. Never," he said.' She ran her finger the rest of the way across Canada to Nova Scotia, where she walked a line across the ocean to Liverpool. 'He seemed changed after that. More determined. When we returned home, he took on the board as investors. He wanted to keep the company growing, and we couldn't do it on our own. Not long after that he started forgetting.'

She stayed focused on the map, and despite the stubborn shell, he felt her vulnerability. He knew the effort of stepping into shoes too big, and Iris, even marvel that she was, must have felt the strain.

'I didn't plan to become dull,' she continued. 'To be tied to this desk. But I blinked, and it happened.' Her fingertips grazed a *carte postale* of Paris. 'And now, he needs me to continue what he started. To see out his dreams, even though he has no idea what they are anymore. How else can I thank him? I owe him so much. After you left, he was all I had.'

A knot in Hamish's throat made it hard to swallow. Sliding his fingers between the smooth lining of his coat pocket, he pulled out the small sepia card that he kept with him, not all the time, but just at times when he felt like he needed a little more luck or comfort. The edges had become tattered from handling it on those long, rambling walks he took to escape a lecture or the suffocating silence. He rarely read it because the words had been memorised, but instead just held it and remembered lighter days.

'After the opera,' he said as he rubbed at its corners. 'You said I didn't look back. And I didn't. Some days, it hurt too much to even think about Honeysuckle Street. But I'm sorry if you thought I had forgotten you. I could never, ever forget you.'

Growing up, she had always been taller, but he stood a few inches over her now. As she looked up to meet his eyes, he was struck by their strength, but also the thin threads of frailty. A faded smattering of freckles across her nose recorded memories of happier times, her face a beautiful reflection of their wild years. He brushed his fingers across her cheek. 'I was sure some man would have charmed you, and I'd have to ask his permission to see you. I couldn't bear it.' He tucked a finger under her chin and brought her lips closer to his.

Like a spark that caught a still smouldering log at morning, the old fire cracked and raced, and nothing, not the sound of the house, the ache in his chest, or the hurt of his memories seemed to matter anymore. Her mouth, supple, yielding, half opened to meet his.

'This is a very bad idea...' Iris exhaled, her breath like a sigh into his soul.

'The very worst,' he whispered as he found her lips again and grazed them with his own. They were as soft as a petal and sweet as sugar water. His body hummed as his mind brought forth images of bare skin and trailing fingers, and an overwhelming curiosity surged in him. Would her thighs wrap around his waist again? Would her body tense and tremble the same? Would her fingernails again dig into his back as she cried out and rocked against him?

Hand on her waist, he tugged her closer as his palm followed the curve of her body until it rested on her breast. Iris gave a little moan, so he stroked his thumb firmer, hoping the pressure of his touch would rub against her, and although he couldn't feel them, he imagined her nipples peaking with desire. If only he could tug her dress open, fold back her bodice, and take one in his mouth...

'Hamish,' she whispered as she slid her hands around his neck. He trailed a kiss over her silken chin, and flicked his tongue over her neck, tasting a hint of rose water cut with salt, a delicious combination that made his desire roar. How could she taste so good? How, even now, was she the most perfectly composed woman he had ever known, when he had known many women, and a good deal more intimately than he knew Iris. The swirl of memories, regrets, fatigue, and emotion crashed as snippets waged a war inside, until one cruel line shouted over them all.

It should not have been Lewis...

'I shouldn't have done that.' Hamish took a quick step back. Cool air rushed between them, and his body felt chill without her touch. 'Returning, it's too much. Too many memories. And my father.'

He was clutching now, and avoided her eyes, scared he might see pain, and instead skated over her beautifully familiar face, lingering on her delicious mouth with its lips now slightly swollen from their kissing. Heavens, how he wanted to kiss those lips until they bruised. He tore his gaze away and snatched his hat from the table.

'I will leave you to your work. Thank you for the lounge. I mean, for the sleeping. I mean, for allowing me to sleep on your lounge.' He was blabbering now. Heat rose through him. He had to leave. Without a backward glance he called, 'Good evening, Miss Abberton,' over his shoulder as he dashed down the stairs, almost knocking Gena into the wall as she juggled a plate of biscuits. He raced out onto Honeysuckle Street and did not stop until he was inside Number 8, his back pressed against the door, panting.

This would not do. He had a plan, and anything more than friendship with Iris was not part of it.

CHAPTER ELEVEN

Three months into her first season, Iris had decided that balls were boring. Even after attending only half a dozen, they became a montage of predictable monotony—the dresses, the dance cards, the ogling. The same boring tunes played in the same predictable order. Time had done little to alter her opinion, and even the novelty of an evening's fancy dress had worn. At least now, by attending as chaperone, she could avoid being lashed into a corset with layers of petticoats, a crinoline, ruffles, and other frippery. Instead, she wore one of her prettier tea gowns that only needed stays and petticoats, made from pink and green silk, and trimmed with venetian lace and beads from Bohemia. She could almost have been sitting down at her desk to work, instead of watching the swirl of the dancefloor.

Iris had agreed to come this evening during a moment of distraction, when her neighbours Elise and Rosanna had begged her to act as chaperone. Rosanna's mother was too ill with her pregnancy, and Elise's aunt had offered, but she was never ready on time, complained about everything, and always wanted to leave as soon as the last dance had finished. As the pair of them pleaded, Iris had remembered what it was to be young and to dream of love, and so she had agreed to accompany them.

And, she hoped, an evening out of her study would distract her from the kiss.

The thought of it caught her in odd moments, like a breath of flowers on the spring breeze or a grain of sugar licked from the corner of one's mouth hours after eating. It had dredged up long pushed down memories and sent stars glittering through her. Damn Hamish. For years she had kept a tight hold on her emotions, and now, one brush of his lips and all the walls she had carefully built crumbled. That one night, so long ago, could have been yesterday.

The earl would never, ever approve of her.

'Mr Babbage is heading this way,' muttered Rosanna to Elise. 'And concealed as a jester. Typical. He is coming to ask me to dance to annoy me; he knows I cannot refuse.'

Iris gave a tired sigh. According to Rosanna's father, Mr Phineas Babbage, who lived beside the Hempels on the opposite side of Honeysuckle Street, had used some trick-ery or bribery to secure the corner townhouse, which had the advantage of extra windows. Mr Babbage denied the accusation, and the petty feud had endured for two years. As the only daughter and her father's favourite, Rosanna had taken on the quarrel with enthusiasm.

Mr Babbage paused before them, then bowed, before extending his hand to Elise. 'Titania. May I have this dance?'

'She's spring.'

'Pardon?' Mr Babbage's head jerked as he looked to Rosanna and frowned, as if noticing her for the first time.

'Spring. That's her costume. And I'm autumn. We match, see?'

'Rosanna, please.' Elise took Mr Babbage's hand. 'I would be delighted to dance.'

'Traitor,' Rosanna mumbled to herself as the pair moved onto the dancefloor.

Iris couldn't help but suppress a laugh.

'Heavens, it's Mr Vincent.' Across the room, near the entrance, the tall, slightly portly partner who sat on the board of Abberton bowed to the hostess, Lady Howard. Almost every day over the past week, Iris had sent a note to Mr Vincent asking to call, and every day he had replied to say he was engaged. Engaged in dalliances and spending the substantial profits he made from Abberton and Co on his mistress, she guessed, but that was not her concern. She felt sure she could secure Mr Collins's vote, and Mr Sanders would agree with a proposal that would make money. Mr Vincent, however, was less predictable. But if she could speak with him first, make her case, he might be swayed. She jostled her way across the room between the throng of attendees before coming to an abrupt halt beside him.

She clasped her hands behind her back and gave an exasperated sigh. Mr Vincent bristled and stumbled slightly over his words. He half turned to Iris, annoyance replacing his supercilious expression, then returned his attention to Lady Howard. A demurer lady would have taken the hint. Iris, however, had once plucked a spider the size of her hand off her father's coat, and she had no intention of being cowed. She shuffled a little closer and sighed again.

'Miss Abberton?' Lady Howard peered around Mr Vincent. 'Is there a problem?'

'My apologies, Lady Howard. I didn't want to interrupt, but you see, I was hoping to dance.' Iris tried her best to look lost, and maybe a little forlorn. 'All the men I know are detained, and the ballroom manager is nowhere to be found. It is not only me. There are many young ladies who have been left to loiter.'

As Iris had predicted, the blood drained from Lady Howard's cheeks. 'Loitering? Oh dear, what will people say?' Her voice edged into a slight panic as she frantically scanned the room. 'Mr Vincent, you must dance with Miss Abberton. Immediately.'

Mr Vincent huffed, but before he could object or make some excuse, Lady Howard raced off, no doubt to scold the poor ballroom manager. He gave a stiff bow. 'Miss Abberton. May I have the pleasure—'

'You may.' Iris grabbed Mr Vincent's hand and half dragged him to the dancefloor. In her haste to force him into conversation, she hadn't even thought to check what dance was next on the program, and she gave a short sigh of relief to hear the opening strains of a waltz. A dance she knew, and one where she could speak with Mr Vincent uninterrupted for a few minutes.

He held her at a slight distance, like she might scald him. The first notes sounded, and half a beat out Mr Vincent pushed forward. Unprepared, Iris took her first backward steps at a stumble.

'I know why you want to talk.' Mr Vincent's steps were sharp and angular, matching his tone. 'It's nothing personal, Miss Abberton, but you should know, I am against it.'

The short speech she had prepared, where she outlined her efforts, her commitment to the company, and how Abberton and Co without an Abberton would be a lie, died on her lips. 'Papa trusts me,' she said as they stepped slightly out of sync with the quartet. She tried to alter her pace to better match his rhythm. 'You know he does. I have assisted him for years.'

'I always said he was too easy handed with you. Should have seen you married instead of traipsing around the world. Now look at you. *Chaperoning*. And his wanting you to take his place is beyond logic, even for Albert. I have no doubt he taught you how to tally a column or two, but business is different. Women are too emotional. Too cautious. They can't make hard decisions and won't take risks.'

When her father had first suggested that it would take time to accustom the new board members to her involvement in the company, she'd been infuriated. She had only backed down because he'd promised that, in time, he would tell them. But time had other plans, and before her father had informed the investors of her role, he had forgotten what that was himself. For months, anger had stirred in her when she thought of his recalcitrance, but as Mr Vincent moved to the edge of the dancefloor, she understood. Her father hadn't been hiding her. He'd been protecting her. What a fool she had been to think they'd accept her as she was.

'At least allow me to present my ideas,' she said, hating that she was pleading.

'Excuse my impertinence, sir, but would you mind if I claimed the next dance?' Hamish gave Mr Vincent a short bow and extended his hand to Iris. He'd come dressed as a highwayman, complete with snug black breeches, black waistcoat, white cotton shirt, and a domino mask.

Iris felt the tension leave Mr Vincent's arm. He extracted himself from her grip and bowed to Hamish. 'Of course, my lord. Although be warned. Miss Abberton does not always keep the beat.'

Hamish took her arm. 'Don't flinch.' His voice rasped soft behind her ear as he squeezed her elbow. 'You're stronger than that.'

Iris took a determined breath, then stepped forward. 'Mr Vincent. Do I have your support?'

He turned with the leisured poise of a man who understood the power of his place in the world with absolute clarity. 'Albert always said you had a good head. And while I have serious concerns, I'll listen.' And without waiting for a reply, he melted into a small group moving towards the supper room.

Elation ran through her as the small victory fizzed in her bones, and it was all she could do not to ignore the slow melody and dance a jig on the spot. They stood on the edge of the dance floor, and her elation faded as awkwardness brewed in the silence between them.

Finally, Hamish broke the discomfort between them. 'This is torturous.'

'I didn't ask you to join me,' she replied, prickling.

'Not you.' He laughed. 'The ball. This is the fourth one I've attended this week. I can't believe I was jealous of you for coming to these things without me.'

'I was jealous you were able to stay home. I would much rather have been drinking tea in Number 6 and telling ghost stories.'

'I was hoping you would say that.' He leaned in close again, his voice little more than a whisper. 'I have come to steal you away. To have some proper fun. Half a block away, there is a club. Cards. Gambling. Invitation only. Care to accompany me?'

'I cannot go into a gentleman's club,' she said.

'It's not that sort of club. And ladies are allowed if they are escorted by a gent.'

'I am supposed to be here as chaperone for Elise and Rosanna.' Still, despite her protest, the old wildness grumbled, malcontent at being shuttered for so long.

Women don't take risks...

'People may notice my absence.'

Far too emotional...

'And I can't be seen in a gambling den, no matter if it allows ladies or not.'

Too cautious...

'All problems I have an answer for. I have already spoken with our good neighbour Mrs Crofts, who was more than delighted to keep an eye on your friends.'

'I have no doubt about that,' Iris mumbled.

'And with Mrs Crofts distracted, no one will notice if you slip away. And your third point... I believe I have the answer.' He tugged at the string of his mask and pulled it loose, dangling it between them. 'A disguise.'

Iris's fingers tingled as she stroked the domino, the black velvet still warm from his body. She hadn't had even a little adventure in years. The most daring thing she did was occasionally ride her horse at a fast trot in the park, but only if it was early morning and she felt sure no one would see her.

'Come be wild again.' He teased as he swung the mask between them. 'Like old times.'

'Less than an hour? You promise?'

'I will have you back before Mr Vincent has opened his third bottle of sherry.'

Iris snatched the domino. 'Which way, Lord La-di-dah?'

Iris's heart thudded with fear, but mostly, anticipation. Hamish kept a tight grip on her hand as he led her down the service stairs and through the laundry, then slipped a coin to the kitchenhand who gave instructions on how to get back inside unnoticed. As they walked at a quick step across the road, weaving between the line of waiting broughams and carriages, Iris kept her head down, as even with the mask she felt incredibly exposed.

The evening had turned warm yellow and orange, and the light seemed to make Hamish glow with fire and energy. His hair, already resisting the restrained part imposed by his valet, reflected gold streaks of light. He tugged her to a stop before a large, brick townhouse.

'Red door,' he muttered to himself as he searched between the house and its neighbour. 'Where's the red door?'

'There!' Iris pointed down a set of stairs to a cherry-coloured door with a gleaming brass doorknocker, her voice far too loud. Now she was away from the stiff ballroom with its regulated order of events, suffocating crowd, and a menu plucked dish by dish from Mrs Beaton's Cookery Book, excitement jumped in her muscles. Their feet cascaded down the stairs, and at the door, Hamish clapped the knocker twice, paused, then gave it three fast claps before standing back. His fingers flexed then curled against hers.

A low muttering came from within. A bolt turned before the door opened two inches. An eye, dark brown with long lashes, pressed itself to the gap. 'We ain't accepting deliveries today,' came the thick Yorkshire accent.

'I am not delivering, only making an enquiry,' Hamish replied. 'Might you be interested in some tulips next week?'

A long silence stretched. The door shifted a little before the man's dark red lips, topped with a thick black moustache, filled the space and spoke in a coarse whisper. 'Wrong flower.'

'Bollocks,' Hamish muttered to himself. 'Roses?' The door stayed unmoving. 'Foxglove?'

'I told m'lord, I told him no one would remember, and besides, it's too bloody hard to pronounce.'

'Chrysanthemums?' Iris offered.

'Hurrah!' The man opened the door wide, laughing, before his face darkened into a frown. 'No ladies,' he snapped.

'But there are ladies right there!' Hamish gestured over the man's head to a small gathering in the corridor. 'Unless half the gents have donned skirts. And I was *told* to have a lady accompany me.'

'Those are not ladies, *per se*. Think of them as...' The doorman tapped his fingers against his chin, 'Lucky charms. Some gents find a pretty face brings them luck.' He gave a chuckle. 'And if she don't, she provides a different type of luck later. Understood?'

Hamish slid a hand about Iris's waist and tugged her into his side. She felt the warm, firm length of his torso, and his strong thighs press against her, each muscle articulated through the thin layers of silk and petticoats. His arm wrapped protectively around her. 'That's what I have done. I've brought my own lady luck.'

The doorman eyed her with suspicion. 'She looks too fancy to be a lucky charm.'

Hamish leaned forward and muttered between clenched teeth. 'Have mercy, man. I decided to treat myself. I've already paid half a crown to secure her for the evening. Isn't that so, my dear?'

Iris gave a small squawk as Hamish pinched her waist. She rolled her shoulders back and leaned into him, laying an overly familiar hand upon his chest. His heart thudded fast under her palm. She stroked his shirt, toying with his collar, and with a vivid flare remembered the thrill of unfastening his buttons. 'I'll behave, I promise,' she said, her voice as alluring as she could make it.

The man's eyes flicked between the two of them, his eyes skating over her dress, before he chuckled. 'I very much doubt you will. But behaving and causing trouble are different things. So, don't cause trouble, you here? Half a crown or no, I'll toss you out in a jiffy.'

The doorman pulled the door wide, and with a slight flourish, gestured down the hall. 'Feisty, that one,' he said.

'Pardon?' Hamish asked as he passed.

'You heard,' the man said with a wink, before he shut the door and dissolved into the dark.

Hamish kept his hand tight around her waist as they moved through the semi-darkness. Every lingering touch between them sent sparks racing under her skin. Before the curtain, a man stepped forward. Hamish muttered something, the fabric pulled aside, and they moved beneath the heavy velvet and into the room beyond.

CHAPTER TWELVE

A roguish thing. He had just given a password and descended a darkened corridor into a gambling den to do a proper, roguish thing. Hamish let the thrill of it fill him. He had entered the sort of establishment his father would never tolerate being mentioned at the table, let alone permit him to visit. Yet here he was, being a *scoundrel*.

Tobacco smoke clung to the ceiling, as thick as fog rolling off the Thames in winter. The room hummed with life and illicitness. Candles flickered from wall sconces and tables, while a fire cracked in the grate. At the tables closest, dice clacked and clattered along green felt for a game of hazard, while behind them at smaller tables, men clutched cards like they were life preserves, and dealers moved their hands faster than conjurers.

Iris leaned in closer, her green eyes sparkling with excitement. In the tight confines of the room, her cologne, maybe cinnamon and rose, cut through the smoke and sweat. That heady mix of sweetness and spice followed her everywhere, and it took all his resolve not to bury his nose against her and drink in the familiarity.

'Where should we start?' A few men he recognised from trips to taverns with Algernon gave him a nod, before their gaze dawdled over Iris for longer than polite. He tucked her closer against his body. 'Hazard is all luck,' he said, a stray curl of hers tickling his chin. 'And I can't be sure the dice aren't loaded. The cards...' he pushed himself up a little to see the tables further back, as he tried to remember the games Algernon and Aunt Tilly had practised with him. 'Faro at the back. Whist, of course, in front. And in the centre, it looks to be *vingt-et-un*.'

'Twenty-one? What are the rules?' she asked.

Interlocking her fingers in his, he led her between the dice games and deeper into the room to stand before a central table, the two of them facing the game, the full length of her body pressed against his. He'd wager she wasn't wearing a bustle, and maybe no corset. No intricate barriers to intimacy, just swathes of cotton and lace between his body and hers. As her lovely arse rubbed against his crotch, Hamish had to think of cold baths, or his father's grumpy old friends, to curtail his sudden urge to throw her petticoats over her head. He could hardly play a serious game of cards with a cock-stand. Slightly regaining control of his desire, he dipped his head so that his lips skimmed her ear.

'The cards must add up to twenty-one,' he continued. 'Court cards are ten, aces are one or eleven, other cards count their faces. Each man plays against the dealer, not each other. If your hand is better than his, he pays equal your bet. Unless you have *vingt-et-un*. If you make twenty-one with two cards, or less than twenty-one with exactly five cards, he will pay double.'

As if in illustration of the rules, one of the players placed down his cards so that an ace faced up and the other card faced down, then he stacked his coins neatly on top.

'That man has twenty-one with two cards. Unless the dealer has the same, he will win double his bet.'

The next man clutched two cards in his hand. He pushed forward a marker, and the dealer slid a card across to him. Hamish could just make out a court card and a six, or maybe seven of clubs. The man picked up the card, then threw his hand across the table with a slight huff, before pushing himself back. He stalked off towards the supper room, possibly to drown his sorrow in free sherry and brandy.

'That man had more than twenty-one, so he went bust. And from the way he threw his cards, it was not his first loss.'

'So the best combination is an ace and a court card?' she asked, her eyes still on the game.

'That's right. And hearts rank highest.'

'Hearts?' She tilted her head slightly, her earlobe close enough to nibble.

'What could be worth more than a heart?' His reply was a breath, and for a moment, the sparkling excitement in her eyes flecked with an awkward vulnerability, and like the evening in her study, the urge to claim her lips infused him. He'd convinced himself the kiss had just been a moment of nostalgia brought on by good biscuits and would soon be forgotten, but with her delectable mouth so close, it took all his self-control to return his concentration to the game. Perhaps he should have taken Algernon's advice and hired a woman for his first, solo excursion. But an adventure without Iris would have felt like leaving his trousers at home: possible, but still completely wrong.

'Drink, my lord?'

A man balanced a tray loaded with dark amber sherry the colour of stale piss, and slightly darker tumblers brimming with what smelt like cheap brandy. *It's free for a reason,* Algernon had said. *Don't let it addle you.*

Hamish plucked a tumbler of brandy from the tray and took a sip. It burned his throat and sent hot vapours through his nostrils, and he had to smother a cough. 'Have you got any whiskey?' he asked.

'Half a shilling a dram, I'm afraid.' The man sniped, and without waiting for Hamish to reply, he moved off to the next table.

Still clasping Iris's hand, Hamish moved to the seat recently vacated by the man who had thrown his cards and set down the offensive drink.

'Minimum a shilling, no upper limit.' The dealer, who was focused on tidying his recently claimed markers, didn't look up. Hamish placed a pile of sovereigns on the table, and the dealer replaced them with a stack of coloured wooden discs. Rough-hewn and painted blue, green, and red to denote their value, they sat bright against the dark wooden tabletop. The dealer shuffled the cards, then dealt to each player, before placing a card before himself. Hamish lifted the corner. A ten.

He suddenly felt at a loss on how to bet. In Aunt Tilly's sitting room, the game had seemed so straight forward. But now, faced with the table and the hard stares of men more experienced than him, uncertainty nipped as all of Algernon's advice crashed in his mind. *Bet high, but not too high. Be confident, but don't be cock sure. Hold your ground but know when to back down.* It all swirled around him, and faced with the confusion of how to continue, he pushed out a single, blue marker to make the minimum bet of a shilling.

Iris bobbed down beside him. 'You should bet more,' she whispered.

Hamish tapped his finger against the marker. Like a child, he'd only been entrusted with a moderate advancement on his allowance, and between drinking and new suits, he had burned through quite a bit of it. He could hardly ask his father for more money. Not that he wasn't prepared to lose his sovereigns, but he needed to lose them right way to garner the most attention.

Iris stroked the back of his neck with her thumb, a light goading that screamed, *trust me*. A shiver ran through him, as warm and intoxicating as mulled wine. 'It's a new deck,' she murmured. 'The odds are good for an ace, or at least a court card.'

Hamish placed his finger on one, then an additional two markers, and pushed them forward. The dealer watched with eagle eyes as all the players placed their bets, then dealt another round. Iris drew a lazy circle on Hamish's nape, as if channelling her patience into him. He pulled the card towards him and tucked it into his hand, twisting so that Iris could see, but concealing it from any onlookers. The queen of diamonds. He stacked his markers in a neat pile on top of his cards before announcing, 'Stand.' The dealer called at nineteen, and Hamish swept his winnings into a small pile. Beside him, Iris twitched with victory and excitement, and when he caught her eye, she winked.

She really was a marvel. When one of the men threw his hand down in disgust, and everyone else muttered about poor play, her eyes flicked over his card, and in his brief glance over his shoulder, Hamish could tell she was tracking them to keep tabs on the odds. Two more good hands, guided by the soft, encouraging strokes of her fingers, and he had almost doubled his buy in. When he became overly confident and went to stack five markers against an eight, she pressed her nails into his skin in silent caution and he reigned in his enthusiasm. They fed off each other, prodding and retreating, speaking in a language without words, understanding one another without needing more than a touch.

Hamish rubbed a six and an ace together, and Iris lightly scratched his skin, and with a delicious flash, the memory of her clawing at his naked back as he entered her returned with explicit crispness. Hamish forced the memory down and tapped the table. A two. Another light stroke, this one caressing behind his ears, and all he could think of was how her heels had wrapped behind him, pulling him deeper. They had been so inexperienced, yet still perfectly in sync. It would be heavenly to feel her lips trailing over his chest again, or to draw her fingertip into his mouth and tease it with his tongue. Because, of all his conquests, nothing had ever resembled the intensity of that first time in the cellar of Number 6.

The dealer raised an eyebrow. Iris twisted a lock of his hair around her finger, tickling beneath his collar. *Sweet mercy*. He tapped the table. A six. One more card under five, and they'd double the pot. Iris trembled against his skin. She was thinking.

The man beside him leaned over. 'How much for your lucky charm?'

'She's not for sale,' Hamish snapped as he toyed with a stack of markers.

'Every woman in this place is for sale,' the man hissed. 'Most women outside too.' His own companion seemed to have abandoned him, as he sat alone. Slumped in his chair, he had the bitter look of a man who had lost too much and was now clutching for a solution. 'I'll pay well because I could do with a little of her *luck*. Unlike the other whores, your lucky charm is not only *incredibly* attentive, she is also the only one wearing a mask.'

To others, the movement would have been imperceptible. But Hamish knew Iris, and with the slight stiffening of her body coupled with the short intake of breath, he felt fear spark in her. He wrapped his arm around her waist and splayed his hand protectively across her stomach. 'As I said, she's not for sale. She's mine.'

'What if I paid you double—'

'I said no! I think I've played enough.' Hamish, protective anger rising in him, flung his cards across the table. 'And your cheap brandy makes me ill. I'd like a whiskey.' Hamish gathered his winnings, and they sat awkward in his palms. He thrust the markers at a passing waiter, who, taken by surprise, fumbled, and dropped a few to the floor.

'Whiskey for everyone!' he shouted. The room dissolved into a frenzy of cheers and laughter as men jostled one another to get to the supper room, calling out, 'Hat's off to you, Dalton,' and 'Cheers, my lord.' Someone passed him a whiskey, which he threw back. 'And as for my lucky charm...' He glared at the man beside him as he drew Iris into his arms. 'I paid good money for her services, and I mean to enjoy them.'

Like slips of silk, her hair slid smooth between his fingers. Greedy with frustrated want, with over a decade of visions of other men mauling her, making her writhe and moan, he clenched his hand into a proprietorial fist, and pressed his lips hard against hers. Whiskey, warmth, and forgotten carefree days, she was the heat that warded off the chill, and his body screamed at him to both run and to never let go.

CHAPTER THIRTEEN

The raucous room dissolved until there was only her and him. Hamish's fingers threaded through her hair, and a slight pain bit her scalp and sizzled hot, igniting the small sparks of want into an inferno. She absorbed him, ignoring the calls and laughter around them, liberated from the weight of all responsibility, even freed of the weight of her silent longing, as the man she had loved for as long as time kissed her with abandon. His tongue pressed, slow, questioning, and she parted her lips in welcome, blazing at his exploration. *It's part of the ruse*, a voice in her mind screamed. Iris adjusted her arms and pulled him tighter. *I don't care*, she screamed back.

'You taste as good as I remember,' he murmured, his teeth catching her bottom lip. 'I've wondered about that. And the rest of you.'

A sharp cough cut through the fog that had enveloped her senses, and with a pang, she felt Hamish tense, mumbling an apology as he pulled away. The man from the door stood before them, a disapproving frown battling with an amused glint in his eyes. 'There are rooms for that, m'lord.' He gave a short nod in the direction of the stairs. 'If you are not in a position to see your lady home.'

'Rooms?' The word came out a pant, his eyes heavy with longing as they tracked down her body, his tongue flicking between his teeth.

'It's what you paid your half a crown for, ain't it?' the man continued. 'Top of the stairs, second on the right. For a small fee, that is.' He rubbed his fingers together, then stretched out his hand.

'I don't have any money.' Slight panic edged into Hamish's voice. 'I spent it all, shouting whiskey.'

Trembling, Iris pulled a shilling from her purse and discretely slid it into the man's palm. 'Thank you, sir. We can see to ourselves.'

She almost couldn't breathe as they stood there, alone yet surrounded. She felt wild again, like the girl who had run through London or climbed pyramids or run alongside trains, not the woman chained to her desk, a slave to the numbers she had once adored.

Hamish kissed the tip of her ear, and a delicious warmth shimmied down her spine, before bubbling in her toes. 'Iris, are you suggesting—'

'Perhaps we should. Just once. The kiss made it clear we have unfinished business. Then, we can go back to our friendship, without all of this curiosity in the way.'

'I have so many questions, Iris. I am intensely...' His voice deepened into a slight growl. '*Curious*. Second door on the right, yes?'

'Yes.' Her breath caught as he grasped her hand and tugged her through the hustle of the room as he made a hard line for the stairs. Men turned with whisps of thanks on their lips, but when they saw Hamish's determined stride, they stepped aside. The occasional snigger followed, but Iris pushed them away, instead focusing on the possessive tightness of Hamish's grip and the hunger in his eyes. Hamish's kiss had thrown her into chaos, and now, the only way she could see to dispel the tension was to see it through.

They took the stairs fast, Iris almost stumbling as she trod on her hem. On the landing, Hamish shoved her hard against the door, the wood biting her shoulder blades as his lips crashed against hers. She drank him in, just as desperate.

'You have sent me mad all night,' Hamish snarled, the scent of bergamot and leather exhaling from him as his teeth scraped her clavicle, his tongue flicking her skin to gooseflesh. 'Those bastards ogling you, thinking they could buy you. How dare they.'

Iris fumbled behind her for the doorknob. As the lock clicked open, the door swung out fast behind them, and she stumbled back until Hamish caught her, and with a few lumbering steps, they bumped against the foot of a wrought iron bed.

Years of wishing and pining guided her fingers to nimbleness in the semi-darkness. He tasted like citrus and sin, fresh and illicit all at once. 'The door, Hamish.' She pushed him away, and with a disgruntled grunt he kicked it closed before scooping her up, raising her onto the bed to collapse into the undulating mattress with its thin cotton coverlet. She plucked his collar buttons open, and as she ran her tongue over the uneven stubble, his groan rattled between the sound of their frantic gasps.

'The wild girl of Honeysuckle Street. Still wild,' he said as he removed the domino and stuffed it into his pocket before yanking her dress from her shoulders, tugging her stays loose and pulling her chemise aside to liberate a breast. 'And still mine.'

Aided by a slip of yellow gaslight infiltrating beneath the door and the spill of moonlight through the thin curtains, Iris's vision became accustomed to the room. As he flicked his tongue across her nipple, circled it until it hardened, Hamish's dark eyes sparkled with lust. As he drew the hard bud into his mouth, first suckling and then nibbling, his teeth scraped the sensitive circle of her puckered areola, his eyelids flickered, his need for her blazing. A groan sent tremors through her, and Iris melted into his ministrations, a slight whimper escaping from her own lips.

'Lord La-di-dah,' she sighed. Hot sparks of want zig-zagged through her. Hamish rubbed himself against her, and through her skirts and petticoats, his hard desire jutted against her thighs. Through his clothes, she rubbed his cock with her palm, and his heavy breath amplified into a needy growl. Encouraged, she unfastened his trouser buttons and slid her hand between the thick wool and soft cotton.

Hamish rummaged through her petticoats, an indecent sound escaping as he oscillated between unrestrained kisses and lewd whispers over small patches of her bare skin. 'I could devour you, over and again.' He caught her lips, his kiss no longer a question but a demand. 'Taste every inch of you. Lick until you beg me to finish you.'

Iris clawed, scrunching the quilt into her fist, as an uncontrollable moan burst out as Hamish rubbed over her drawers, his fingertips dancing between her thighs. Grunting in frustration, he tugged until the tie loosened. Iris wiggled it down, caught the waistband with her toe and kicked it loose. She kissed the dip behind his ear and wrapped her fingers tighter around his cock. Hamish slid a strong finger between her folds, the light gesture such a sharp contrast to his heavy want and his relentless mouth that Iris bucked beneath him. Each finger flick sent a torrent of burning pleasure radiating through every pulsing muscle.

'Do your other lovers stroke you like this?' His hot breath raced across her cheeks. 'Do they make you moan like I can?'

'Do yours?' she shot back, pulling him closer, her hand working faster over his stiffness, the stab of jealousy through her as visceral as the bitterness in his tone.

'There is no one like you.' Hamish took her breast in his mouth again, lightly biting, as he slid a finger inside, his penetration gentle and deep. He withdrew, then rubbed her again. 'You are so damn wet.'

'More,' she begged, her thighs widening. How long since she had felt such a connection, such intimacy with another, instead of the suffocating loneliness of her own attentions with nothing but memories to excite her. Hamish plunged in two fingers, his thumb rubbing at her nub. Iris felt powerless to do anything but take, the feelings an explosion burning to an inferno inside her. She found his mouth again, savouring the salty tobacco-tinged taste of him.

From the edge of her pleasure, Iris registered a tap on the door. Hamish tensed, his movements slowing, his body turning away from hers in distraction. 'Sorry to interrupt m'lord, but we've had a tip-off. The coppers are on their way.'

'Police?' Iris propped herself up on her elbow. Hamish gave an anguished grunt, then withdrew his hand from between her skirts. He sat up, sliding towards the edge of the bed, absent-mindedly fastening a loose button as he stood, before tucking his cock into his trousers. Iris followed, her breath still gasps, the sharp zinging in her body slowing as the fluttering need between her legs faded. The delirious bliss subsiding, and blinking fast to regain her bearings, she steadied herself against the curved iron of the bedstead.

'How long?' Hamish called, his focus still on her exposed breast.

'Maybe ten minutes,' came the fading reply before the man's feet clattered away down the hall, his step heavy on the stairs.

A disgruntled anger simmered, not only at the interruption, but at being thwarted in her quest to break free. When would they have another chance like this?

'Fuck me, Hamish,' she puffed into the shadowy silence. 'Fuck me like tomorrow doesn't exist.'

Hamish, who had been refastening his collar buttons, paused. 'Ten minutes,' he muttered, then, with an anguished cry, he grabbed her skirts and jerked her close. He sat back on the bed, pulled her onto his lap, and bunched the cotton ruffles of her skirts and petticoats. With a determined tug, he steered her to straddle, his fingers no longer gentle but probing. 'Ride me,' he said as he unfastened his trousers and guided his hardness to her. 'I can't spend another night full of questions.'

He thrust into her, fast and demanding. She howled at the sensation of him filling her so deep and desperately, her guttural groan bouncing off the walls. Every inch of her body hummed with delight.

Iris jerked her hips, seeking his rhythm, but with her knees balanced on the edge of the mattress and her arms wrapped around his shoulders, she struggled to find purchase. She felt suspended over an abyss, and her body tensed with each awkward movement. Each time he sunk into her, she curled away. Completely out of sync, they both became increasingly frustrated as they butted against one another. The beautiful memory of their first coupling, when they had moved in harmony, retreated, and Iris was overwhelmed by the disappointing awareness that this excursion had been a very bad idea.

'Hamish…' Her voice came high, almost wheezing. Fingers dug into his shoulders, her clamouring failure suffocated as it rushed and swarmed inside her. 'I can't hold on, I can't—'

Hamish braced one hand against her back, entwined his other through her hair, and drew her face close to his. 'I won't let you go,' he whispered against her lips. 'Trust me.'

Layers of fabric and lace scrunched as Hamish's promise morphed into a kiss, his tongue inquiring, and Iris followed his lead. She relaxed, and as her weight eased into his strong splayed hand, his grip tightened, and she remained steady. Instead of clutching for balance, she settled into him, and the control that she craved in every part of her life disappeared. She rose along the length of his cock, letting his body guide her movements, before sliding down over him, his firm shaft filling, her fears dispersing as the earlier lights of pleasure sparkled to life again. With her face buried against his shoulder, she felt the old connection between them renew. Their wordless way of understanding, of knowing without asking, it all returned. Iris shifted closer, Hamish thrust faster, and in response, she rolled her hips to match his pace, a whimper accompanying the shudder of delight created by the change of momentum. In the half-light, she etched the rough stubble on his chin, the glinting moisture on his brow, his lips half parted, his eyes wide with passion and wonder, all beautiful fragments she snatched between each plunge of his body into hers, and each crack of heaven that ripped through her. When it became too overwhelming, she had to shut her eyes to keep everything inside, and as the intensity began to swallow her, she stuffed the back of her hand against her mouth to quell the grunts she could no longer contain.

Hamish knocked her hand aside. 'Louder.' He inhaled her with a kiss, before breaking free with a breathy gulp. 'Roar, my wild girl,' he said, his forehead pressed against her. 'Roar for me.' The rough stubble on his chin rubbed coarse, and he pinched her nipple hard, and the flash of pain clashed with pleasure, heightening every sensation until she wailed, lost in the crest of her ecstasy as it peaked.

The hot, glorious rush of electric energy pounded between them. Rigid and trembling, her hips made small, ineffective thrusts as tremors tore through her, and she became lost in the torrent. Tight as a spring, she stayed cramped against him until the final whisps of her orgasm fluttered and faded, and the battering euphoria was replaced with the warm glow of satiety.

With a deft roll, Hamish flipped her onto the bed, tugged her to the edge of the mattress, grasped her waist, and thrust hard. His pounding against her throbbing wetness was almost painful, but also beautiful, and she drew in the vision of his face contorting with each buck until, with a final cry, he pulled out and spilled against her thighs, his breath a gasp, followed by a whisper of, 'Iris, you are magnificent.'

For a moment she lay sprawled as he fumbled in his pockets, retrieving a handkerchief to wipe her clean. As he helped her to her feet, voices rumbled and shouted beneath them, and a heavy pounding intruded through the building.

'Oh no, the police.' Panic rose thick and fast, and she scavenged around the room searching for her discarded pieces. 'Where is my purse? My drawers? I can't be caught somewhere like this, I can't.'

Hamish fastened his trousers, then grabbed his waistcoat from the floor and shrugged it on. 'We've got time. Trust me.' Even in the darkness, she could make out the calm mischief in his eyes. The shouts downstairs distended. With a devilish grin, he pushed the window sash open before clambering out, his feet swinging from the ledge.

Iris peered over his shoulder, her hand resting on his bicep. He swivelled to steal a kiss. 'It's a short drop. I'll catch you,' he said, then he pushed himself off and landed on the stone patio below. Iris shimmied out after him. Her feet hovered mid-air, and without a glint of hesitation, she dropped after him. The rush of cool air over her cheeks hummed with the memory of carefree days, like the rush of wind off the sea or the gust of a passing train, until Hamish caught her, gathering her against him as her legs wobbled.

He didn't let go, just held her, his palms flat against her back and his chest pressing against hers. She thought he might kiss her again, and fear curled at the notion, because if he were to, she didn't think she would ever be able to fold him back into the small square she'd locked him into all those years ago. But he made no motion, except for his eyes, which searched hers. 'Do you feel free?' he asked, his face troubled. 'Are all your questions answered?'

'You are completely out of my system,' she replied, forcing her voice steady.

The relief in his exhalation stung the air.

'How long have we been gone?' she asked, smoothing her skirts.

Hamish flipped open his watch and squinted. 'A little over an hour. We best return before you're missed.'

In a dark corner of the garden, and with a surety she chose not to dwell on, Hamish helped straighten her petticoats, tighten her stays, and neaten her gown. Police thudded past, and they skulked along the back alleys, until they reached the main street. Before the tearooms, they separated without a word, merely exchanging a glance before

Hamish blended into the throng. Iris spotted Elise and Rosanna scanning the foyer, the two of them muttering. She slipped in beside them.

'Where were you?' they snapped in unison.

'I was mending a tear in my dress,' Iris said as light as she could. 'We had best get you both home.'

Once enveloped in the carriage, Iris pulled her shawl tighter. As Elise and Rosanna nattered about which debutante had the nicest dress, and Rosanna complained about Mr Babbage, Iris took a breath and let it evaporate from her, but try as she might, the memory of Hamish refused to be folded back into the compartment of her heart where she had kept him all those years.

Rather than freed, she felt more trapped than ever.

Chapter Fourteen

Hamish's body jolted with each stride of his horse's gallop. His breath laboured ragged and undisciplined, while low branches stung his scalp, but no matter how hard he rode, he could not jolt himself free of the previous evening. As he slowed his mare to a walk, the memory of Iris's touch still lingered on his skin.

Her nipple that puckered under his tongue had tasted soft and sweet, like honey-soaked figs, and the thought of them sent an exquisite shiver through him. But what did the rest of her taste like? If he placed a trail of kisses down the centre of her body, over the delicate softness of her stomach, grazing his teeth over her hips to flick his tongue between her folds, would she moan the same? He loved the taste of a woman's honeypot, yet, in his haste, he had not even thought to give hers a cursory lick, and last night, in his lonely bed in Number 8, the question of how a delicacy like Iris might taste had plagued him. No matter how many times he flicked at his curtains to stare at hers, he couldn't stretch his imagination to bridge the gap in his curiosity. The question tormented him, as if knowing the answer would settle all the uncertainty that had ever swirled within him before.

Algernon pulled up his horse beside him. 'What devil is chasing you? I said a friendly race, not a mad cap gallop.'

'I have been in the country since I was eighteen. Why would you think I needed riding lessons?' Hamish snapped.

'My intention was to teach you how to make a day-light spectacle, and you would have if you had gone slow enough to let anyone recognise you.' Algernon watched Hamish from the corner of his eyes. 'Nursing a sore head? Was last night a success?'

They trotted the horses across the road until they arrived in front of Aunt Tilly's. Hamish dismounted and passed the reigns to the groom's assistant, a scruffy boy of maybe twelve, who had been waiting for them out front so that he could take the horses around to the stable to water them.

'No point being coy about it, as we've established, I am not your father. I am in your life to be precisely the opposite of him. I was merely going to say good show.'

Hamish avoided Algernon's quizzical look as he rapped against the door. An uncomfortable shiver ran up his spine as they ascended the stairs to Aunt Tilly's sitting room. He'd gone to the den to make a flamboyant scene over cards, to launch his reputation as a rogue, not to seduce Iris. But the memory of her face contorted in pleasure as the most luscious moans of ecstasy spilled from her lips shuddered through him, leaving him warm and wanting. Could he do that to her again? If he took his time, would she writhe against him more than once in a night?

At the sitting room door, Hamish waited to be announced as Algernon swaggered in. Once inside, he found that the room had been transformed into a fabric warehouse. On the table, the lounge, over the rug, and spread by the window lay swatches and bolts of linen. Quigley stood to attention in the middle of it all, three tape measures draped around his neck. Two boys, one of them the messenger who had delivered his waistcoat the week before, waited to one side, shuffling from foot to foot.

'What is all this?' Hamish questioned his aunt as he kissed her cheek in greeting. He placed his hat and gloves on the table beside a swatch of blue and red ginghams. His foot nudged a basket of folded slips of satin, and in the centre of the room, an open trunk disgorged multicoloured tweeds over the floor.

'Rakes do not get about in suits that could double as mourning wear.' Algernon took a seat by the hearth and stretched his legs.

'I could have gone to the tailor,' Hamish said. 'There is no need to bring the tailor here.'

'Nonsense, boy. You are not to be inconvenienced, you are a rake, remember? Quigley has orders to make you a new wardrobe. The brighter, the better. But not too bright. The goal is to be noticed, not to resemble a peacock.'

Hamish had never thought much about clothing. When he was young, he had worn mostly Lewis's hand-me-downs, and after the accident, his father had sent him to the local man for his needs. Hamish stroked a swatch of cotton. Emerald green and flecked with shimmering golden thread, it was almost the same colour as Iris's eyes. 'Can I have a waistcoat in this?' he asked.

'You can have anything you like, my lord, provided you settle your expenses. Unlike some.' Quigley's gaze drifted to Algernon, who gave a short cough.

'Put it on his account,' Algernon muttered, then clapped his hands. 'Tell us your story, Hamish. No details glossed over. We want to know *everything* about your evening.'

'There isn't much to tell.' Hamish raised his arms when Quigley nudged him. The tailor ran the tape measure around his chest, then from his shoulder to his hips. 'We played cards, we took a good haul, and I spent it all on whiskey. Things pretty much went to plan.'

Quigley took the roll of green fabric and shook out a length before draping it over Hamish's shoulder. Then, he scurried to the far end of the room and dragged back a roll of navy plaid and thrust it at Hamish, who grasped it with his free hand. Quigley took the end and tugged until it spilled onto the floor. 'Can I suggest this for trousers?' He took a length of sky blue and draped it over Hamish's shoulders. 'Some subtlety in the shirt.' Finally, he shook out a roll of terracotta coloured wool. 'And lastly, a coat in this.'

Hamish tried to look down to get a sense of the colour combination that had excited Quigley so much, then looked about for a mirror.

Algernon paced before him a few times, arms crossed and one finger tapping against his lips. 'Not common, that's for sure. But not too outlandish either. What about a brighter waistcoat?'

'The waistcoat is already too gaudy,' Quigley sniped.

'What do you think, Aunt Tilly?' Hamish called across the room. 'Too bright, or not bright enough?'

Perched on the lounge, Aunt Tilly scrutinised him. He had always thought of his father and aunt as polar opposites. But in her shrewd stare, he realised that not only did they share the same eyes, but the same perceptive mind.

'What do you mean, "we" won at cards?' she asked, her voice light but sharp.

Hamish fumbled for words. 'The lucky charm I took. She was—er—very good luck.'

Algernon's head turned, like a bloodhound sniffing the air. 'Your whore helped you at cards?'

'Don't call her a whore!' Hamish snarled. His aunt and Algernon's expressions shifted from amused interrogation to shock. He hadn't meant to snap at them. 'Sorry, I didn't sleep well. I can't stop thinking about her,' he confessed.

'Why didn't you make use of the upstairs rooms?' Algernon asked. Hamish burned hot, and before he could sputter an excuse, Algernon started to snicker. 'You did! I heard a tale of a gent scampering out a window! You cad!' Algernon slapped his knee, still laughing. 'Never fear, you poor besotted fool. The solution is simple. Just buy another night. Arrange a room at the Langham Hotel, make like rabbits, and be done with her.'

'I can't.' Hamish ground his toe into the floor. 'She wasn't paid.'

'A lady?' Tilly asked. 'Someone's wife? Or a debutante?'

'Neither. Not a lord's daughter, I mean, not nobility, but still kind of is... you know what I mean.' As Quigley circled him, readjusting the bolts of fabric, swapping terracotta for indigo, then bottle green. Hamish tried to get a handle on his thoughts. 'I've known her for a long time, and she was always just, you know. A friend.' He was babbling now, he knew it, but the feeling of unburdening the conflict in his chest felt liberating.

'Not your neighbour?' his aunt asked. 'Abberton's daughter? I remember the two of you as children. Practically lived in each other's pockets. But she's so prim. You took her to a gambling den?'

'Prim? Not Iris,' he chuckled, then quietened. 'She was amazing. At cards, at—' he bit off the intimate confession he had been on the verge of spilling. 'I've never been so captivated by a woman before. Yet I've known her forever. It's just all so confusing.'

'Come on.' Algernon stood and buttoned his coat and grabbed his hat and gloves from the table. 'Time for another lesson.'

'Where are we going?' Hamish scooped up his own apparel.

Algernon rolled his eyes. 'To have some sense knocked into you.'

Hamish's muscles ached and his cheeks throbbed as he pulled himself up the rough trunk, wedged his foot in the tree fork, and hoisted himself to sit on the wide oak branch that stretched before Iris's window. A soft yellow light drew a thin line around the curtain edges. She was still awake—most likely working—and hopefully in need of a distraction. With one hand braced on the trunk, he leaned out and tapped a knuckle against the glass.

'Go to the laundry, Spencer,' Iris said, her voice a muffled monotone. 'I am too busy to rub your belly.'

'What about mine?' Hamish called.

The curtain split as Iris appeared at the window. Annoyance turned to shock. She wrenched the sash up and leaned out.

'You've been hurt? What happened?' she asked.

Hamish brushed the cut below his eye. 'A friend took me to a boxing match. Turns out, I am about as good at boxing as I am at drinking. And horse racing.' He swung his legs idly, scared to meet her eyes, but when he looked up, all he found was concern. 'Can I come in?'

Iris held out her hand, and Hamish clambered through the window. Inside, the room smelt of sweet tea and ginger, and with a fire burning low in the grate, it felt like a warm embrace. Iris shut the chill night out and tugged the curtain closed. Her dressing gown slipped open to reveal a small triangle of skin and the slight bump of her collarbone. How had he not thought to kiss that exact spot when it had been exposed to him the night before?

'After the match, we went to Haymarket,' Hamish explained. 'My friend thought that if boxing hadn't helped cure my distraction, then a lady or two might.'

Iris stiffened and scrunched her collar closed. She leaned against the desk and tucked her feet beneath her, like she might disappear amongst her books.

'I think this conversation is beyond the boundaries of friendship. Or at least, a friendship with me,' she said.

'I couldn't do it,' he said, chancing a step closer. 'I couldn't even look them in the face.'

Iris stayed bunched and guarded. Even though she worked in her night clothes, her hair remained pinned up from the day in a loose, although now slightly untidy, bun. A finger tapped at her collar while her brilliant eyes remained downcast, as if fascinated by the rug. He willed her to look at him like she had the night before in the den, when she had melted into his arms and confessed that she wanted him. Maybe, she had told the truth when she said he was out of her system.

'I can't stop thinking about you. About last night,' he said.

Her eyes flickered and finally met his. 'Nor can I,' she whispered.

Emboldened, he slid his hand under the thick quilt of her dressing gown and skimmed the soft, thin cotton beneath. Unlike the night before when her body had been masked by layers of fabric, he could now caress her hip, feel each soft indentation of her ribs, and enjoy the heat pulsating from her. 'My curiosity is far from satisfied. Quite the contrary, I find myself raging with questions.' He tugged her and she glided forward, the aroma of lemon soap and fresh linen enveloping his senses. 'And as amazing as last night was, I feel we were far too hasty to rid me of my inquisitiveness.'

She pressed her cheek against his, as soft and delicate as the flower that shared her name. 'What questions do you still have?'

Hamish untied her dressing gown and pushed it from her shoulders. 'I want to know, if I kiss you, right here...' He found the little bump of her collarbone he had spied before and stroked it with his fingertip. 'Will you like it? Will you giggle, like the ticklish girl you were? Will you squirm? Or some other response entirely?' Hamish skated his lips over the undulation. The lightest sigh puffed from her, along with the hint of a whimper.

'We can't continue like this,' she said, even as she kissed his cheek, chasing his mouth until she caught it.

'One last night,' he countered. 'Just one. Because if I have to spend my life speculating about the taste of your honeypot, I may not sleep again.' Gooseflesh shuddered over her skin as he drew her night gown over her supple thighs to reveal the soft curl of her womanhood, light brown and tinged with fiery copper. He tugged off his coat and let it fall to the floor before dropping to his knees. 'Because I am bordering on obsession. I must know; does it taste as delectable as the rest of you?'

Her thighs widened at the slightest nudge, and the scent of sex and woman that he had reluctantly washed from himself that morning filled his next breath. He wanted to ravish her, but with a pinch of his nails into his palm, he forced himself to slow. Iris was a rarity to be savoured, because, as she had hinted, this night was all they had. She would move on, with Abberton and Co, with her conquests, and her adventures. He was destined to return to his perpetual habitation of Lewis's shadow. At least here, with her, he felt himself standing in light.

He began at her knees, at the point where her flesh indented, before moving to her gorgeous, full thighs and her lovely, round bottom. At first, only grazing the soft flesh with his mouth, he inhaled the avenue to her most intimate place, before his resolve cracked, and he began to lick and mouth at her like she was a meal to be devoured. With his tongue, he wrote her name and his, like children carving initials into a tree trunk, before he moved to her centre and slid his tongue between the most decadent folds of her slit. He grasped a firmer hold and tugged her closer, burying his face deeper. His tongue ran in slow, lazy circles, her sweet saltiness better than any draught he had drunk in any bar. Needing air, he rested his cheek against her silken thigh. 'You taste like heaven. But then, a goddess would taste like heaven, wouldn't she?'

To his delight, Iris gave a long, throaty groan, and tipped back a little, her body arching, her free hand stretching behind her to keep her balance. She tangled her fingers through his hair and guided him back to her most sumptuous heat. His tongue flicked, and her clit firmed.

Iris began to thrust her hips, each little movement accompanied with an increasing moan. Hamish continued to lap and lick. She could have been cursing or calling his name or both, but everything came muffled as her thighs clasped tighter against her ears and she clutched his hair, pushing him firmer against her. She was so wanting, so knowing of what she needed, that Hamish momentarily shrunk from her vitality and had to fight the urge to retreat, lest he disappoint her.

'More, Hamish,' she demanded. He slipped a finger inside, slow and controlled, as she had enjoyed him doing the night before prior to their interruption. His tongue worked rapidly. He felt her climax build, and he meant to drink down every damn drop.

The moment she tipped from want to orgasm, from pleasure to release, from grinding to fucking his face with abandon was nothing short of glorious. All he could do was call her name into her wetness, until her breath came in small gasps, her chest swelling and ebbing with each exhalation. In the maelstrom, he hadn't registered the ache in his knees, but he felt no regret. To feel her unravel, to taste her, had been worth any discomfort.

When the last of her little jerks against him quelled, and her fingers loosened from his hair, he raised himself a little higher to rest his chin on her pubis bone.

'One last night, my wild girl?'

With a light flutter, her eyelids opened, and she ran her thumb over his bottom lip. 'Yes,' she gasped, then lunged. Her mouth colliding against his, and the thought of her tasting her own pleasure made his cock throb so hard, he thought he might spill before he had unbuttoned his trousers. 'No unanswered questions. I want you to ask me every last one.'

Chapter Fifteen

Iris, this is a very bad idea.

The words came from the last skerrick of common sense she still held. After tonight, he would leave, like always. He would find a bride of the right status, return to the country, maybe never come to town again. She would be left with nothing but the anguish of his absence. All day she'd tried to stuff the memory of the night before down by focusing on her preparations for the presentation, failing dismally. After all, it had taken her years to fold Hamish into a neat square and lock him in a discrete compartment of her heart. If one small, heated moment left her befuddled, what would become of her after an entire night? His proposition was a very, *very* bad idea.

If this is so bad, why does it feel so good?

More than good, he felt exquisite. Not just the magic he worked with his tongue, or the ferociousness of his kisses, but that he looked at her the way she'd always fantasised. From the way he licked his lips, to the gravelly undertone in his whisper, she knew that he finally saw her as more than a playmate and a friend. He desired her as a woman.

'What is your next question?' she asked, toying with his waistcoat buttons.

Hunger burned hot in his eyes as he ran his palm over her waist, lightly cupping her breast and stroking her nipple with his thumb. An expectant quiver ran through her. He bowed his head and kissed her there, his hot breath radiating through the fabric. 'You like this, don't you?' Hamish trailed his tongue over her clavicle, caressed her nape with his lips before nibbling her ear lobe. 'I remember.'

Nimbly, Hamish plucked the pins from her hair, until her bun cascaded free. He tickled his fingers through her curls, loosening her braids, the light scrape of his fingers over her scalp sending the most delicate warmth through her, and with it came the realisation that tomorrow, everything would change. By sundown she'd likely be a member of the board, a woman who filled her life with columns, percentages, and tallies. Tonight, for just one final night, she could be the wild girl he still imagined her to be.

'You used to have a scar over your knee,' he continued, inching her nightgown up. Did it fade?' He brushed his thumb over the knotted sliver of skin, the light caress making her tingle. 'Split your knee as we ran through Hyde Park. Refused to cry, although I know you wanted to.' He took hold of her hand and walked the few steps backwards to the hearth. 'What else about you is different. And how are you the same?'

As he went to remove her nightgown, Iris lightly swatted his hand away. 'I have my own questions,' she said, unfastening his waistcoat. 'You used to be thin enough to squeeze through the kitchen window. But I'd wager you look a little different now.'

Hamish nuzzled her neck, his mouth alternating between hot kisses and whispered obscenities. She worked his buttons loose and pushed his shirt from his shoulders before tugging his undershirt over his head and discarding it on the floor. He tasted of exertion, and lust, of an adventure into a part of the city she no longer dared to descend into. Country life had made him hard and strong. Firm, smooth pectorals, a flat stomach with a slight sink to his belly button, and a thin, dark line of hair that disappeared beneath his waistband. When she enclosed her lips over the small bump of his nipple and teased it with her tongue, Hamish groaned.

He drew lazy circles along her back, tracing each vertebra. 'How many of these darling bumps of your spine can I feel.' His breath came as a pant as he worked fast at his trouser buttons. 'How many can I count?'

Hamish kicked the last of his clothing away, and before she could grasp her nightgown hem, he took hold and levered it over her head, too fast for her to protest or prepare herself. A shimmer of fear shuddered through her. Time had made him a man, but it had made her a spinster. No longer the belle but a chaperone. The young, strong maid from his memory was long gone and had been replaced by a woman who spent too many hours seated at a desk. Her hips had rounded, her breasts were a little less firm and supple, her legs a little more dimpled.

The hiss of embers in the fire filled the silence. 'I am not the girl you left,' she said, her eyes still pinched closed as she girded herself to meet Hamish's disappointment, but before she could move, his lips collided against hers, as hot and devouring as the night before.

'You most certainly are not,' he growled. Iris gasped as Hamish slid his hand between her slit, quickly finding her nub and stroking it with the same deliberate, delicate touch. 'How are you so flawless? So fucking delectable?' The sudden surge of electricity, of desperate want, almost made her buckle at the knees, and she clutched for him, half limp with longing. 'Turn around,' he ordered, twisting her as he spoke. The strong lines of his body undulated around the soft curves of hers. Hamish gripped her chin, tipping her head so that she rested against the firm broadness of his chest.

'Do you always close your eyes when a man enters you?' he whispered, his cock nudging at her core. Iris groaned and nodded. His hold on her tightened just a little. 'Open your eyes. I want you to look at me as I take you.'

She thought she might be lost forever in the orange glow of the coals dancing in his piercing gaze. He thrust, fumbled between her legs, and then, with a sigh, slid inside her. Despite his jealous questioning, and her bold avoidance of his interrogations, she had never known another man but him. How could she when he possessed her so completely? As he thrust again, gaining confidence, the two of them finding the others rhythm almost instantly, the blissful throbbing radiating through her, she knew that she was conquered. There would be no compartmentalising and moving on now. Her only hope was to surrender to the torrent of him, capture every spark and sliver she could, and keep the memory to warm her the rest of her wretched days.

'How is it you feel so good?' Hamish grasped her hips, and Iris had to brace herself and widen her stance to hold her balance. His thighs slapped against hers as he propelled himself into her, harder, faster, deeper, so excruciatingly pleasurable that she forgot her awkward hold on the mantle. He pulled out, spun her around, and with a jumble of limbs and lips, the two of them tumbled to the floor.

Hamish made to roll her onto her back, but Iris placed a staying hand against his chest. He allowed her to push him to the rug. She swung one leg over his torso, straddling him as she had the night before.

'You wanted to see me?' Iris raised herself up a little and guided his cock to her entrance while holding his stare, the raw sexual energy and ecstasy mixing with the furious victory that now, after all these years, he wanted her so desperately. 'Here I am. Tell me—what do you see?'

His penetrating look broke as she lowered herself onto him, and he pushed his head back into the rug with a heavy sigh, his eyes half closing as his fingers dug into her thighs. His deep penetration urged on the most delicious explosion of turbulent harmony. He grunted, and she moaned alongside him, the two of them reduced to an animalistic enjoyment of one another, composed completely of sweat and slip and salt. Iris scraped his ear with her teeth, and Hamish bit her nipple so hard she gasped with pain and shock, their rhythmic coupling amplifying the sensation. Pleasure rose and bubbled as the first moans of climax began to form, and Iris let her body run headlong into it, instinct and desire vibrating through her. Hamish wound her hair into his fist, then dragged her down, their faces barely an inch apart.

'I see *you*,' he said, then pressed his mouth hard against hers.

As he gifted her earlier release with his mouth, he stole this one the same way, and Iris had no choice but to breathe each pulse of ecstasy into him. She longed to scream out her pleasure, but Hamish remained unrelenting in his hold on her, and instead, her moans remained muffled against him as each racking tremor coursed through her, until she collapsed against his chest, puffing against his neck, enveloped by their scent of sweat and sex.

Hamish rolled them over, then plunged into her, hot and unrestrained. 'My goddess,' he growled. The solidness of him blocked out everything, and with the last of her climax slipping to a dull ache, she melted against the rug. His passion unbridled, he grunted and thrust with recklessness. Iris drank in the sight of him—the slant of light across his face, the rapture in his expression, his body taut as he bucked, all of it for her. Barely half a dozen strokes and he groaned, and with a half-smile, watched his seed spill against her stomach.

Like the night before, Hamish cleaned her quickly, then drew her against him to snuggle into his side. He stretched out his arm, and she rested her head against his chest as he draped his arm over her. Between the warmth of his body and the heat from the fire, she felt completely ensconced in a cocoon.

'How are your questions now?' she said.

'Many are answered, including some I didn't even ask. You minx.' He nipped her wrist before planting a kiss. 'But there is one thing I've always wondered. And while I could happily bury myself in your luscious body looking for an answer, I doubt I'll find it there.'

'Maybe I should make you go hunting for it, just in case,' she teased.

He chuckled, her head bouncing slightly with his laughter before he quietened. The air took on a serious edge. Her heart, already slowing, squeezed tight, like they stood on the edge of a precipice.

Finally, he spoke, barely louder than a whisper. 'Why did you give yourself to me? All those years ago?'

'You gave yourself to me too,' she said, forcing her voice to remain light even though she parried her question as a shield. 'It was simply a trade.'

'But not an equal one. Maybe, between us, but not to the world.'

The words and the weight of the love she had carried with her, never fading even through his long absence suddenly felt very heavy indeed. To let them out would be to ease her burden, but also, it would change everything, and even though everything was already changing again, she reigned in her fear and bit down on the few small words she ached to speak *because I loved you and still do*, and buried them inside.

'Because—' Even her next breath felt heavy. 'Because I knew once you left, you wouldn't come back as Lord La-di-dah, the ignored second son. If you ever came back, you'd be heir apparent to the earldom. And while many ladies would throw themselves at Lord Dalton, and he would take some beautiful, titled bride, Lord La-di-dah would always be mine. Hamish, the forgotten boy of Honeysuckle Street, would stay with me.'

A dark curl fell across his eyes, and curse her, her fingers trembled as she pushed it back. He frowned in contemplation, then realisation.

'There are no other men, are there? No lover on every continent?'

'Just you,' she whispered, her lips against his. 'There's only ever been you.'

Words became superfluous then, and kisses replaced questions. Stretched and warm, unburdened at least a little, they found one another, much as they had all those years before. The fire in the grate burned to embers, then died, and in the semi-darkness they rocked together, slow and searching, until they knew everything there was to know. His weight pressed against her, they gasped and whispered into each other until, as aching with pleasure as she had been, she roused again, tensed, and shuddered beneath his strength. As she wrapped her legs around his body, he pressed himself deeper, spending himself in her as he whispered, 'Iris, my wild girl,' against her cheek. And when the grey of morning intruded, they finally separated to dress, and before the window held each other until a lark sang, and this time, kissed each other goodbye knowing there were no more questions left to ask.

'There's something you should know. About the mission my father sent me on, and my plans.' Hamish spoke haltingly, as if wrestling with the words as he swung himself around on the branch.

'Not tonight.' She couldn't bear to hear the name of his future bride, be it Lady Tatton or Miss Wade. No doubt she'd read it in the papers soon enough.

Hamish nodded; his expression conflicted. He nodded at the desk. 'The board would be mad to not appoint you. You're the most magnificent person I know.'

She leaned out the window and caught one final kiss before wrenching herself away. When he reached the ground, she tugged the window closed and watched as he walked the short distance, following his silhouette until he disappeared inside Number 8. And like always, he didn't look back.

Chapter Sixteen

Waking after lunch, following an exhausting night making love with a beautiful woman, had to be the best imaginable start to the day.

Although, as Hamish washed his face, he reflected that waking up beside a beautiful woman and fucking her speechless would have been a *better* start.

He shot a look out the window as he wondered what Iris was doing now. It must almost be time for her presentation to the Abberton board. To that slime Mr Vincent, the pompous Mr Sanders, and that fool Mr Collins. Surely, despite her necessary deception, they understood how hard she had worked for them all these years. Surely, they weren't so blind that they would fail to see her brilliance.

A knock on the door shook him from his thoughts, and Hamish stilled. He'd only mumbled the occasional, 'Not now, Irving,' as his father's valet had tapped at the locked door all morning, and now, fully awake, Hamish shied from the prospect of enduring yet another of the man's curt lectures, delivered verbatim via a letter from his father. Hamish had only received one direct correspondence since he had arrived: a short note requesting a list of potential brides. Hamish had left off his reply as long as possible, before finally sending back the names of ladies who had attended Elise's tennis fundraiser—leaving out the thoroughly suitable Lady Miranda and Lady Felicity, of course.

Irving knocked at the door again, this time more insistent, and called, 'My Lord? Are you well? I've received a communication from your father. There's something we must discuss.'

Hamish had arranged to meet Algernon at Aunt Tilly's for instruction on how to play skittles in a rakish way, and he had no desire to listen to another lecture. He checked himself in the mirror, then swung a leg over the window sash and reached for the branch. 'I think I may have a cold. Or one of those viruses from the Thames that's in all the papers. Don't come in.' He didn't bother waiting to hear Irving's reply.

Aunt Tilly's butler didn't bother ushering him up to the sitting room to announce his arrival. Hamish was glad of it. He felt twisted, and this afternoon, any hint of propriety grated. It all reminded him of his overbearing father. He stripped his gloves as he entered the sitting room, searching for his aunt in her customary seat by the hearth, but she wasn't there. Despite its silence, the room held breath, and it wasn't until his eyes adjusted to the indoors light that he spotted her tucked onto the window seat. 'Aunt Tilly?'

When Tilly turned from the window, the sunlight angled stark across her face. Thin lines of tears streaked her cheeks, and she wiped beneath her eyes and turned away, but too late to hide them from him.

'Tilly? What's wrong?' Hamish strode across the room to his aunt's side.

'Your exploits have reached the estate.' She held out a note. No, not a note. A telegram. Hamish took it and scanned the paper, and with each cutting phrase he could imagine the old man, bent and bitter, carving the words with his pen like he was carving his name into the desk with a pen knife, before sending a messenger to have it telegraphed *post haste*. It must have cost him a fortune to send his diatribe, but knowing the old man, he would have considered it a worthy investment.

CEASE YOUR ASSOCIATION WITH MY SON.
TRUMPED UP STRUMPET.
NOT MY SISTER.
YOU WILL NOT HARM THIS FAMILY FURTHER.

'He never was one for eloquence.' Tilly's eyes brimmed with tears. 'I can't say I'm surprised. I expected as much as soon as you came to call; I just didn't expect it to hurt so much.'

Hamish's fingers slackened, and the paper fell limp. Tilly shied away from it like it could burn and turned her face back to the window.

'He has no right.' Fire, hot and angry, burned raw in him. 'Bitter, twisted old coot. All he cares about is propriety, but he doesn't have one shred of decency. But how did he know?'

'Good morning one and all, good morning. No champagne? Are we not celebrating?' Algernon swept into the room, his coat tails flapping and his grin as wide as the doorway. His gaze flicked between Hamish, to Tilly, and his smile morphed into a frown. 'Have you seen *The Tattler*? I thought you'd be elated. I was beginning to have my doubts you could pull it off, but it seems you've created quite a proper scandal. No names, of course, but there can be no doubt it's you.'

Algernon seemed to move in slow motion as he shook out the paper and crossed the room. Hamish's mouth went dry, his tongue a clammy lump in his mouth as his heart beat out a staccato rhythm. He couldn't move, and instead of taking the paper from Algernon, he only leaned over to look down at the short articles grouped together under the bold heading 'Fashionable Faux Pas.'

Anything but 'Dull'
A young lord returning to town for the season and finding himself attracted to less gentlemanly pursuits is not a new story, but one that is usually carried out with a certain amount of discretion. Perhaps influenced by his aunt, the notorious Miss T, the young lord's behaviour has proven to be anything but dull. He recently attended a makeshift gambling house, where he showed significant luck at the game, then narrowly avoided a police raid by escaping out the win-

dow with what the men of this club call their 'lucky charms'. But perhaps this lord did not need luck or even his winnings, as we have since received reliable information that she is none other than a certain Miss A, adopted daughter of a wealthy businessman with exceedingly deep pockets...

Fury exploded in Hamish's chest, and his fist clenched before he walloped Algernon on the cheek. 'What did they pay you?' he bellowed.

Caught off guard, Algernon stumbled before straightening himself. 'Steady on,' he said as he stepped backwards, putting a chair between them. Hamish strode forward, pushing it aside, his fist tensing in anticipation. 'I didn't tell anyone. You were the one prattling on in front of the most indiscreet tailor in London.'

Hamish exhaled as if he'd been winded. 'Quigley?'

'That's part of the package. An expertly made suit, a horrid waistcoat, and the right rumour circulated. That's what you wanted, isn't it? I thought you knew.'

Hamish flopped onto the chair. After so many botched attempts, he had finally pulled it off. A right proper scandal. The name Dalton dragged through the mud. He could almost hear the doors closing against him and feel the rumble of his father's fury.

The elation bloomed, then withered as dread curled in his chest. 'Oh no. Iris.'

He almost tumbled as he raced down the stairs, two at a time. As he wrenched the door open, Algernon's shouts followed him, not intended as a taunt, but hounding him, nonetheless. 'My boy, what did you think a scandal was?'

Chapter Seventeen

She was going to be late. She couldn't be late.

'Gena, have you seen my gloves? I wore them yesterday. I swear, they were in my room.' Iris pulled back the curtains and then lifted a cushion on the lounge.

The clock struck the quarter hour. In less than thirty minutes, she was expected at Abberton and Co London Offices, and if she was going to make it in time, she needed to leave five minutes ago. 'Sans gloves it must be then,' Iris mumbled to herself. She gathered her folders and papers into the crook of her arm, gave her father, asleep in his chair, a peck on the cheek, then made for the stairs. Perhaps if she spoke in the same flat monotone and focused on the numbers, no one would notice her naked hands. Or perhaps they'd be so taken with her ideas, and when she showed them how hard she had worked these past years, it wouldn't matter. After all, the men of the board wouldn't be wearing gloves.

A thump on the door echoed through the entry.

'No callers Mason, I am already late,' Iris called from the landing as she spied her gloves on the stand. She juggled the papers to snatch them and tucked them into her pocket.

She could slip them on once she was in the carriage and on her way.

The knock came again, louder and more insistent.

'It's Mr Worthington,' Mason said as he opened the door. 'He doesn't normally visit on a Friday.'

Once unlocked, the door flung back and slammed hard against the wall. 'Where's Iris?' Jonah demanded, his eyes darting before they settled on her. He took the steps fast, and when he reached her on the landing, he clasped her into his chest. 'I came as soon as I heard.'

'Watch my dress, Jonah, you'll crush the ruffles. What has gotten into you?' She disentangled herself from his hug and smoothed her blouse. 'You will have to tell me later, for I am late. I am presenting to the board this afternoon. Will you wish me luck?'

The colour drained from Jonah's cheeks and concern, even fear, replaced the panic. 'You don't know.' He thudded back down the stairs and yanked the front door open. 'Is he there? I'll kill him. I'll bloody well kill him.'

'Jonah!' Iris took the stairs slow as fear wrapped cold tendrils around her spine. 'What are you talking about.'

Jonah ran his fingers through his silver flecked hair. As he ascended to the middle of the staircase, he reached into his coat pocket and pulled out a haphazardly folded broadsheet. He started to open it, then shook his head and passed it across, his expression pained.

Iris, fingers shaking, reached for the paper, her heart racing even though her stomach had turned to lead. She didn't have to read the entire article to understand what it was, and who it referenced, and the horrible implication of it all.

'He's caused a scandal,' Jonah whispered. 'But why?'

'To agitate his father,' she replied. The evidence in her hands collided with her memory of when he had arrived at the house drunk, claiming he had a surprise for the earl. Had he planned this since his arrival? Surely, he wouldn't take the magic of their nights together and turn them into something sordid. She could scarce believe it. But then, he had never taken the task of finding a wife seriously. She'd thought him just blowing off steam and enjoying his freedom. The entire time, had he been plotting to use her to injure his father's name?

'We can sue for defamation,' Jonah said, his hand warm on her shoulder. 'If it's not true.'

Iris scrunched the paper into her fist. 'And what if it is?'

A rap on wood broke the painful silence. Mason, in his confusion, had not closed the door, and in the entry stood Mr Sanders, who brushed off his hat and tucked it under his arm as he stepped over the threshold with a copy of the same paper in his hand. 'It's true then. You visit gambling dens and have secret lovers. Abberton and Co will not tolerate a reputation like this. A woman on the board is one thing, but a woman with loose morals? No one would trust us. Our stocks would plummet.'

Iris's grasp on her folders loosened, and they tumbled from her hands. Invoices, tallies, and her handwritten notes erupted and scattered over the stairs. A few light sheets swirled before settling in the entrance at Mr Sanders's feet.

'Mr Sanders, this is completely unfair,' she pleaded. 'This is one minor thing. One indiscretion.' She bent as best she could in her stiff corset and formal dress, the bustle impeding her movements. Mason stepped forward to help, but Mr Sanders snatched the notes from him, and in a few sweeping movements, he had gathered up all the disparate pieces of paper.

As he straightened with her documents, Iris saw not just weeks of work, but years of her life clutched in his strong arms as he sneered up at her. 'Minor? I think it's a little more than that! The board will not stand for such behaviour.'

'Such behaviour?' Anger bloomed in her chest, like a caged animal that had become frustrated with its confines and now demanded to be set free. 'I am hardly unique in making such a slip. Mr Vincent has mistresses on Bond and Grosvenor Streets. Mr Collins spends every cent of his profits at the races. And you...' She didn't know anything about Mr Sanders, but that likely just meant he hid his secret better than his colleagues. 'You'll have some proclivity. Some weakness. You all do. You demand we women police you for it, and then carry the burden of it when you fail.'

Mr Sanders held her stare. 'I can assure you, Miss Abberton, that you will not find my character so besmirched. Ever!'

'Jonah? Iris? Why all the shouting?' Papa shuffled onto the landing, his dressing gown thrown over his suit. He clutched the banister and, with a slow rock, eased himself down the top stair. 'Is it time to go to the theatre? I cannot find my hat.'

Jonah leapt the few steps to tuck his arm into Papa's side to keep him steady.

'Take him to the sitting room,' she said to Jonah, but too late. For all his faults, Mr Sanders was an astute man, and comprehension lit his eyes as he looked from her notes, to Papa, and then her.

'The board has already met.' Mr Sanders swelled with self-importance as he spoke. 'We reject your application to become a member. And given his clearly deteriorating state—a condition you have obviously connived to keep secret—we will likely revoke his position too.'

'You can't take this from us,' Iris gasped. Hot tears swelled in her eyes. 'Abberton and Co without an Abberton? It's preposterous.'

'You will still receive your share of the profits!' Mr Sanders snapped. 'But as to the running of the company, we will find someone more—'

'Wait!' Unshaved, dishevelled, and not wearing a hat, Hamish's broad body filled the doorway and blocked out the sunlight. He gripped the frame, then half bent, panting. Mr Sanders jostled to the side, gripping the folders tighter, his expression as calculating as a fox. Jonah growled, but Iris silenced him with a look.

'Have you come to gloat?' She took a few stiff steps down the stairs. 'Enjoy the carnage you created?'

'I didn't mean for it to happen like this, you must believe me. I would never hurt you. I've come to set things right. Iris, marry me.'

As Hamish dropped to one knee, he fumbled in his pocket before withdrawing a ring and extending it towards her. A stray beam of sun glanced off a facet and splashed a shard of light onto the floor. She didn't have to be closer to know it was his mother's, and before that, his grandmother's ring. After all, she'd seen it before.

Iris stopped, suspended, with one foot hovering over the stair and her fingers gripping the banister as she sought to keep her balance. The household, who all seemed to have made their way to the entrance, even Mr Rogers from the back stables, gawped, their heads turning from Hamish, to her, and back again. Mr Sanders clutched the papers closer to his chest as he watched the exchange, possibly weighing the cost of his outburst on future opportunities.

A million times as a girl in her bed, she had imagined a future where Hamish found himself free of familial obligation, and where he looked on her not as a friend but more. And while in the fantasy her father did not mumble, 'Who is that man in the ugly waistcoat,' the sincerity of Hamish's words were every bit what she had imagined.

'But what of your father,' she said as she planted her foot on the next step. 'He would never approve.'

'I'm counting on it,' Hamish said with a laugh. 'I can't believe I didn't think of it before. He will be livid. Marrying you is a far better revenge than any scandal I could hope to concoct on my own.'

Chapter Eighteen

If words were rope, he would have hauled them back in. But they weren't, they were whisps of noise and air, and once released they couldn't be retracted any more than smoke could be stuffed into a bag.

The small glow in Iris's eyes disappeared like a candle flame snuffed out. When she finally spoke, her voice came quiet and cold.

'Revenge?'

'I mean, he would not approve of us, would he? He would be outraged if I married someone inferior.'

'Inferior?' Her voice went up an octave.

'I don't think that. You know I don't. That's just what *he* would say. You've always been my friend. My equal.'

Hamish shuffled a little as the wood bit his knee. His arm fatigued as he stayed statuesque, the diamond ring his father had begrudgingly sent him to town with stretched into the cavity between them. Above him, Iris stalled.

'I think you do believe it.' Her words cut the silence; her tone full not of her warmth but cold awareness. 'And you would wield me like a weapon, hoping to shock him and his friends. You would make enemies and walls for our children before they were born. You would wear my, my...

inferiority like a pin on your lapel, a proud reminder to others of your bold choice. That is not my choice. I will be your scandal, but I will not be your revenge.'

She looked slightly lost for a moment, her fists at her side, her eyes damp with tears as her gaze flicked between the papers in Mr Sanders's hand and the diamond in his own. She turned in a slow semi-circle and, with her hand clasping the banister, took a step up.

Iris had never walked away from him. It had always been he who left, and as he watched her climb, his stomach jellied as fear ground through him with an intensity he felt through every bone.

'You love me!' He meant it as a plea, but instead, his words shot out like an accusation. He pushed himself to his feet. 'And I... I think I love you too.'

When Iris turned to face him, her love was writ on every line of her face, as it always had been, so obvious that only a dolt like him would have missed it all these years. Pure, strong love mixed with anger and determination, her beautiful complexity streaked across her every feature.

'I do, Hamish. I always have. And if twelve years has done nothing to cure my stubborn heart, I can't imagine a lifetime will change things. But I have grown used to carrying my love for you as a burden, not a lightness. Every time you left and didn't look back, I became a little better at holding its weight. Maybe it's time you learnt what that is like.'

With a handful of skirt bunched in her fist, Iris continued to the landing, where she took her father's arm.

Hamish stepped on the bottom stair, but Mason put a restraining arm before him and barred the way.

'Leave it, my lord,' Mason said in a low voice. 'Even if you make it by me, you're not likely to get past Mr Worthington.'

'Iris, please. Please!' The words tore from him, and with each syllable, he felt his heart shred and leave his body to follow her. He grasped at air, called her name, but with each light tap of her foot, she moved further away, and she did not look back. In as much time as it took for Mr Sanders to humph out the door, Iris's skirt hushed across the landing and out of sight.

The walk from 4 Honeysuckle Street, past the vacant block of Number 6, felt like a journey through infested swamp lands, or a cursed cavern. Hamish watched his feet as he moved, and it was only when he paused by the stairs that led to the entrance to Number 8 that he took in Irving waiting by the carriage. Hamish's trunks had been strapped to the roof, and the driver sat upright and waiting, the whip twitching with anticipation.

'Are you ready to leave, my lord?' Irving opened the carriage door, the small steps unfurling. 'Your father has sent instructions.'

His father. The man who ignored him until he decided he needed him. Who controlled his every breath, yet still couldn't stand him. Hamish chewed on the memories as his old fury revived. 'Have you always been so insufferable, Irving?'

'I am sure I don't know what you mean.' Irving's eyes narrowed. 'My lord.'

'I mean, does my father deliberately hire pernicious men like you, or does he turn you this way.'

Irving held his glare. 'I have a family. They rely on me. My opinions and thoughts are irrelevant.'

Hamish's stomach twisted in disgust. Not at Irving, but at himself.

He really was no better than the man he professed to despise. Maybe he was worse. After all, his father merely acted a part in the world he knew. He had always been the first-born heir and had lived a strict life of that expectation. Hamish had known freedom, and love, and he had chosen to throw it away, and for what? Revenge for his lost youth? As he turned to Number 6 and looked across the vacant lot, the truth became as bare as the exposed rubble. He loved Iris, had always loved her, because to know Iris *was* to love her. He hadn't acknowledged it not because she was beneath him, but because she shone so brilliant, so much brighter than he deserved.

Irving coughed and nodded towards the carriage. 'Best be on the road, my lord.'

'Everything is packed?' Hamish eyed the trunks strapped to the carriage roof.

'Yes, my lord.'

'My notes? And—'

'All of it, my lord.'

Hamish looked across to Number 4. He put his boot on the carriage step, and with his hand on the rail, hauled himself up.

'I always liked Miss Abberton,' Irving said, following Hamish's gaze. 'She reminded me of my mother. Tough as an old boot and as soft as a lady's shawl all at once. We all knew what you two were up to.'

'We weren't "up to" anything, we were friends!' The suggestion that their entire relationship would be judged by that one sordid article grated.

'I didn't mean that, I meant when you were young'uns. Sneaking about town, getting into mischief, but never mean or nasty to anyone. It always gave us a laugh to see what you two would get up to. Everyone in the street thinks the world of Miss Abberton.'

'Everyone in the street?' Hamish looked past Number 4 to the ornate columns of Odette's villa, then shot a look across the road to the Hempel's home, Mr Babbage's, and even Mrs Croft's, where he could see her nose twitching at the curtains. Hamish twisted to look to his neighbour, the duke, whom they called the old grouch even though he was their age, and for all his grumpiness, he had still allowed Iris and Elise to use his lawn for their fundraiser. Iris was the only woman he had loved; he saw that fact now as clear as the thick strips of cloud across the blue sky. But then, *everyone* loved Iris.

'I've been an arse,' Hamish said.

'Your words not mine, my lord,' Irving replied.

'And Iris... she didn't deserve what I've done to her.'

Irving bit his lip, not quite meeting his eye.

'I can't change the past, but maybe I can make things a little better. I have an idea, but I need a few hours to pull it off.'

'And when you're done, you'll climb in the carriage and head back to the estate, as your father orders?'

'I promise. Not for him, but for you. And your family. I respect that.'

Irving tilted his head thoughtfully. 'What did you have in mind?'

Chapter Nineteen

After seeing Papa to his favourite chair, and reminding Jonah she was never one to fall into vapours, Iris took herself to her room, but sleep would not settle. After tossing for more than an hour, she finally dressed in her favourite tea gown and made her way to her study. There, she slumped into her chair and swung idly, her eyes misting in and out of focus at the piles of notes, ledgers, and correspondence piled on the desk. All the papers that had suffocated her life over the last few years. All information Abberton and Co would need to ensure a smooth transition from her work to whomever took it over. She shot a look at the fireplace and thought to burn the lot, but then dismissed the idea. While Mr Sanders and the board could go the hell, destroying records would disrupt work and hurt the employees and their families that relied on them. And the board likely knew they would be her weakness—that was how men like them won out over people like her. She cared too much.

Instead of thrusting it into the fire, Iris began to stack the Abberton paperwork into neat piles and tied them off with white ribbons. Part of her wanted to rage across London and holler at the men who had taken her work from her, or ask them to reconsider, or to even beg them to allow her to continue in secret. But with each sheet of parchment that she placed into a folder, the weight on her shoulders shifted.

Iris slumped back in her chair, and she looked across the desk, past the notes to her father's empty seat. The memory of their days in here, passing ledgers between them, arguing over invoices, discussing sales and markets fell hard and heavy. She burst into tears.

Keeping the books for Abberton and Co had ceased bringing her joy for some time, but the hope of keeping alive those days when Papa had been lucid and sat opposite had always spurred her on. But Jonah was right. He saw it clearer because he knew her father better than anyone, and in his visits each week, he saw the stark change that she herself could not face. Releasing Abberton and Co felt like he slipped a little from her, but she knew clutching to a memory would not help them through the challenges ahead. He needed a daughter with fortitude and patience. Not a daughter with her head consumed by tallies and lies.

In the soft afternoon light, flicks of dust motes shifted and swirled in a shaft of light that lit his chair. She could almost see him looking up from his papers and pushing his spectacles up the bridge of his nose.

'I miss you.' Her voice cracked at the recollection of him as he had been, the man still alive and napping by the fire in the room next door, but somehow, still gone.

The memory smiled and turned towards the map on the wall, the way he always did when a letter about some tile in an exquisite shade of bluc or some expert rug weaving

technique reached him, and his eyes twinkled with anticipation as he planned another adventure. Iris turned to the
wall, trying to follow the glimmer of where he was looking,
but couldn't quite place it.

Who was she to be now?

Iris, I give you the world.

'Miss Abberton?' Mason stood by the door. 'Some people are here to see you.'

'Please no callers Mason. Today has had enough excitement.'

'These aren't callers, exactly.' Iris scrutinised his face,
searching for a clue, but the actor's mask held firm. 'I think
yourself and Mr Abberton would call them potential investors.'

Curiosity waged a war with frustration as she walked
down the stairs. Mason ignored her questions, until he
paused at the threshold to the front parlour and announced, 'Miss Abberton will see you now,' like she was
the queen and not some upstart from the streets who just
happened to be good with numbers.

'Odette? Elise? Rosanna? Why are you here?' Iris tore
her gaze from her friends seated on the lounge to sweep
around the room. 'Mr Babbage? And Mr Hempel?' While
their backs were firmly turned on one another, they were
amazingly in the same room, and even more amazingly,
silent about it. Iris looked to the tall man by the window,
his features a little indistinct in the half-light. 'Your grace?'
Indeed, it was the Duke of Osborne, who never called
on anyone on Honeysuckle Street and kept his London

activities confined to his villa, his club, and parliament. 'Why are you all here?'

'To hear your proposal,' Duke Osborne grumbled. 'Dalton's valet was most incessant. Be quick. Some of us have other engagements to attend to.'

'My proposal? Mason, I—'

A rap came at the door, and Mason shot down the hall and tugged it open to reveal Mr Sanders, holding one of her folders, and flanked by Hamish and another man she didn't recognise.

'I do not wish to see you,' Iris hissed as she hurried towards them. It was bad enough that the household had seen her humiliation. She did not need it seen by the street.

'And I do not wish to be here,' Mr Sanders said in a curt voice.

'I was speaking to Lord Dalton. Although, I have no wish to see either of you. And you,' she looked to the other older man dressed in a waistcoat as ugly as Hamish's. 'I have no idea who you are, but if you are in company with Lord Dalton, I am sure I have no wish to make your acquaintance.'

Hamish winced as if wounded, still not meeting her eyes.

'Algernon Pascoe.' The other man removed his hat and bowed. '*Enchanté.*'

'Lord Dalton and Mr Pascoe,' Mr Sanders spoke between gritted teeth. 'Suggested I return these to you. They arrived at my offices with some acquaintances of theirs, some *ladies of the night*,' he hissed. 'They threatened me with scandal. Me!'

'Gabriella and Luciana are not ladies of the night,' Algernon tsked. 'They have been retired for some years now. It's not my fault men like you judge before you know a person.'

Hamish nudged his elbow into Mr Sanders, who jolted forward. 'These are irrelevant to the future of Abberton and Co.' He thrust a folder at her, much thinner than the one he had left with. Then he brushed Algernon's hand from his coat, gave her a curt nod, and stomped down the stairs.

Iris flicked the folder open to find pages of her handwriting: her notes for the presentation, financial predictions, and the numbers she had run on a business idea that would take the company in a new direction. An idea too big to achieve on her own, but with the right investors supporting her, a venture she could make a success.

'I don't know what they'll say.' Hamish nodded down the hall to where half the street sat waiting. 'But I wanted to give you back your chance, the one I took from you. And here.' He reached into his pocket and pulled out a key. 'You don't have to take it, but I wanted to invest first. You can use Number 8 for lodgers, people coming in from out of town who need somewhere to stay. I can't imagine I'll be back for some time.'

'It's too much.' Their fingers brushed as she took the key, the familiar sizzle racing through her.

'For what I've done, it's not nearly enough. Now go tell them why Irving has asked them to wait in the parlour all afternoon. They have no idea. Goodbye, Miss Abberton.'

'Goodbye Lord... Lord Dalton.'

Mason had closed the door before Hamish and his friend had reached the bottom of the stairs. A cough sounded down the hall, followed by a dissatisfied grumble. Iris looked at the folder. The toes of her boots rustled her skirt as she entered the parlour. She took a steady breath, taking in all the people assembled. Neighbours. Friends. Even Spencer the cat, curled on a chair. Some people she'd known her whole life, and, she hoped, people who would see past a scandal if they saw value in the opportunity beyond.

'Good afternoon, ummm...' How to address them? They ran the gamut from your grace to spinster miss. 'Good afternoon, Honeysuckle Street. I have been working on a business proposition for some time, and—'

Elise caught her eye and motioned her hand up, her mouth forming the word *louder*. Iris cleared her throat. 'As you all know, Papa and I travelled anywhere we could. His dream was always to bring the beauty of the world to London, and to place it within the reach of ordinary men and women. Just a little piece.' Iris remembered the spark in her father's eyes when he planned another trip, and the passion with which he spoke of sales and pay rates and opportunities. 'But he didn't live through things. He lived through experiences and adventures. And I wonder, if maybe, we could create a business for people like him. People who want more than just a shot of lace from Venice, or a handmade tile from Egypt. What if, instead of bringing a hint of adventure to London, we gave people an adventure of their own?'

Iris spoke from her heart, even beyond her heart, from her soul, of those moments that had resonated with her. Of the beauty of a waterfall at sunrise, or the splendour of a sun sinking behind a mountain range. Even during the terror of having their baggage stolen and hopping a carriage, she had learnt how strong she could be. She wanted them to understand how travel wasn't only about discovering places, but of discovering oneself.

'And that is my idea,' she said, pacing before the fire, her notes long since discarded as her enthusiasm took over. 'To take people by road, or train, or boat or any means necessary, not just to see things, but to have adventures! Wonderful, life-changing, mind-boggling adventures. Not quite as rough or unexpected as those Papa and I had, but something with a little more edge to them than they might find elsewhere.' She turned to the room, spread her arms wide, and exhaled the last of her breath into a smile. 'What do you think?'

For a moment, she thought her talk had bored them to stone, as all of them sat stiff and unmoving.

'You've worked very hard, I can see that,' Odette spoke slowly, no doubt choosing her words carefully. 'But what would you offer that a tour with Mr Thomas Cook does not?'

'Thomas Cook offers amazing options, but I am not talking about being in competition with him, *per se*, although as Papa says, "Every player in the market is in some sense a competitor."' *Back on track* she chided herself. 'I am talking about special tours. Like an itinerary of grand structures for the engineers. The Champs-Élysées in Paris for the newly minted heiress in need of a fresh wardrobe who is too afraid to ask for guidance, lest she seem an idiot in the eyes of the *ton*. Historical tours for scholars, or a focus on... on... I don't know, libraries and bookshops for the reader!' She dared a look at Odette. 'Even the chance to visit opera houses and attend concerts with a famous soprano as company?'

Rosanna's father leaned over the arm of the chaise to retrieve one of her sheets of paper. 'I'm not so certain about the viability of such an undertaking—'

'I'll invest!' Mr Babbage called out abruptly with a sharp look at Mr Hempel. 'I believe in you Iris. Always have.'

'I wasn't implying I don't believe in her,' Mr Hempel half rose from his seat. 'I was simply asking a question.' He dropped the papers onto the table. 'I too will invest.'

Odette shrugged. 'What good is money if one cannot use it to raise up a friend? I am here for you, my darling, but I will *not* be leading a tour.'

'It's some years before I come into my majority,' Elise said. 'Maybe I can help with the books? Or the advertising? I know how to plan an event.'

'Oh Elise,' Iris pressed the back of her hands to her eyes. 'I would love your help.'

'You are all quite mad!' The Duke of Osborne turned back from the window and huffed, his hands on his waist. 'People have been travelling to the Continent and beyond for centuries without assistance.'

'Excuse me, your grace, but you mean people like *you*,' Iris spoke gently. 'People with family or connections, people for whom letters of introduction can open doors. But others do not have the same luxury. Papa and I travelled to all these places. I know the best places to stay, or to try a local delicacy, or where to find the most striking scenery. But I also know where a young lady can have a dress mended in a hurry, or the best place to have a hat made.'

'You are all being frivolous.' The duke crossed his arms. 'Lucky for you, I can afford to be frivolous from time to time. I will make a modest investment.' He pouted a little, gave a sniff, but also added the hint of a smile. 'And if anyone can make this ridiculous idea a success, you can, Miss Abberton.'

Iris tried not to burst into laughter, although doing so would have provided a welcome release for the elation bubbling inside of her. This afternoon she had imagined herself condemned to this street, now, in a short span of time, it had proved her salvation, even better than salvation, because instead of being beholden to hypocritical old snodgers like Mr Vincent and Mr Sanders, she would be accountable to her friends and neighbours.

'What will we call ourselves?' Odette asked. 'No offence, my dear, and I genuinely do say this with all sympathy, but, given recent *events*, the name Abberton may not encourage the right type of bookings.'

'What about Honeysuckle Street Travel company?' said Mr Babbage.

'That name,' said Mr Hempel. 'Is terrible.'

'What about Spencer and Co?' Elise scratched behind the old tom's ears. 'He's seen parts of London we can only imagine, but no matter how exciting a night he's had, he always comes home. That's what it's all about, isn't it? The joy of departing, and the joy of return.'

As if in approval, Spencer stretched his legs and pawed at the air, arched his head backwards to expose his neck, and gave a rumbling purr. Rosanna smiled, Mr Babbage chuckled, and even the duke gave half a grin as Elise tickled Spencer's chin.

'Spencer and Co Travel. Adventure and excitement with the comforts of home,' said Iris. 'Elise, it's perfect.'

Chapter Twenty

The carriage pulled up at the entrance to Caplin House sometime after midnight. The lamps cast eerie shadows over the gravel drive, the meagre light accentuating the moss-stained teeth of the sandstone gargoyles that perched over the oaken double doors. The dim light stretched their shadows over the bricks, so that it appeared as if their wings were spread, and the monsters were about to swoop from their perch and devour him.

Hamish stepped onto the gravel and arched his back into his knuckles, his spine cracking with the movement. The monsters hadn't scared him even as a child—they were far less menacing than the demon inside. He trudged up the stairs and raised his fist to knock like the visitor he always felt himself to be, but when his knuckles hovered inches from the door, it swung open, and one of the staff—he could never keep track of their names, so many of them fled to better employment once subjected to his father's tirades—stood to attention and gave a short nod.

'Welcome home, my lord.'

Caplin House must have been the only building in England where, even in the depths of winter, outside was warmer than inside. Hamish tugged his coat around him as he walked into the entrance, his breath misting before him. He was about to ask for a warming whiskey to be sent up to his room when the familiar hunched form lumbered across the landing and paused at the top of the stairs.

'You went and bollocksed that up, didn't you?' the earl barked.

If Hamish had been wearing his hat, he would have doffed it and bent into an exaggerated bow. As it was, all he could do was plant his feet and meet the old man's glare. 'Spectacularly,' he replied, the *-ly* reverberating off the stone floor and walls.

His father grunted, silencing the echo.

On the journey, Hamish had consoled himself that he had made things right with Iris, and from what he had taken, he had given back as much as he could. He had lost Iris before he knew what she meant to him, and while it was a poor consolation, he would still, at least, have his revenge. But as he rolled his shoulders back and met his father's penetrating stare, the freedom he had craved eluded him. He had made a mess of things, and in doing so, he had not scandalised the old man at all. He had simply proved him right.

'The tenants need attention,' his father grumbled. 'See you're of a temperament to visit them in the morning.'

He shuffled off, his long shadows converging into the night. After he had gone, Hamish turned to the man on the door, thinking of the whiskey, then decided against it. The coldness, while not a comfort, felt like what he deserved. A penance for his stupidity.

Spring arrived, then stretched into summer, before retreating to make way for autumn. Rich reds, oranges, browns, and russets adorned the trees, which slowly dripped their leaves onto the lawn. A cascade of auburn to taunt him, for as Hamish stood at his window each morning, contemplating his day as he sipped his morning chocolate, all he could draw into his mind was the image of Iris lying before the fire, her hair streaming behind her, the flames casting an orange and yellow glow over her skin. Part of him craved winter so that he could be done with the memory, but part of him dreaded it as another loss. In a year, would his reminiscences goad him the same? Was there a way to get her out of his system?

Hamish didn't turn at the tap at the door, only called, 'Enter.'

'Do you require help with your coat, sir?' Since their return from London, Irving had resumed his duties as his father's valet, but had developed a habit of calling on Hamish each morning so that he arrived at breakfast before the old coot, thereby avoiding a lecture on punctuality. Not much of an alliance, but a small kindness that, for its briefest appearance, helped him feel a little less alone.

'Thank you, Irving. I can manage.' Hamish took his coat from the back of the chair and tugged his arm into the sleeves.

'You have also received an invite, my lord. From Viscountess Tremaine. She was hoping you might help her with her tennis serve. Her husband, the viscount, is away for business, and she is...' Irving coughed. 'Frightfully bored.'

Hamish spun to face Irving. 'Frightfully bored?' While they'd never discussed it, the phrase was practically code for *come visit and fuck me senseless*, an activity he'd regularly enjoyed before he left for London. After only a few years of her marriage, the pretty young wife was already neglected in favour of a mistress, having supplied the necessary heirs and dowry.

'The messenger said it twice. *Frightfully bored.*'

Hamish toyed with the days schedule. His father had asked him to inspect the tiles being laid at the village church, but he could put it off. The change would annoy the old man but cause no harm. Tomorrow would suffice. An energetic game of tennis followed by an energetic afternoon in her chambers might help blot London from his mind, if only for a short time.

Hamish turned back to the window. The maple closest to them shivered as a slip of aggressive wind swirled across its branches, tugging dry leaves free and sending them swirling in a torrent of red and orange.

'Please send a note back to the viscountess explaining that I am detained in the village, and likely will be all week.' He was Lord Hamish Dalton, future Earl Caplin. And instead of fighting that, he needed to accept it. And like the boxing, or the failed trips to Haymarket, an afternoon with his lonely neighbour would not help with his preoccupation. Iris was entwined with him and would forever be under his skin. He had to learn to live with her there.

'And if you please, my lord, you have a delivery.'

Irving held out a small *carte postale*, like the one of the aqueduct that he kept tucked in his pocket and carried with him everywhere. Mail was normally placed on the breakfast table, along with *The Times*.

Hamish took the card and turned it over in his hands. On the picture side, a photograph of the Arc de Triomphe in Paris beamed up at him. On the reverse, he recognised the script, but let his eyes stay soft so that he could savour the connection and anticipation of what might be written there.

L'Arc de Triomphe has 284 steps.
Gena grumbled about every single one.
Amazing view.
I hope you can see it one day.

'Were you going to hide this from me if I took up the viscountess's offer?' Hamish asked.

'That would be grounds for immediate dismissal. I would never be so derelict in my duties.' Irving adjusted his cufflinks. 'I may have waited until you were at breakfast to deliver it though. But given your preoccupation with the changing season, I thought you may appreciate a quiet moment to read it. I must see to your father. I'll make sure he takes the stairs a little slower today.'

Hamish tucked the card into his pocket, beside the older one. The new card sat stiff and unyielding, but in time, it would soften to his body. Today, as he made the short journey to the breakfast parlour, he liked the slightly awkward feel of it in his pocket as its corners jutted at his chest.

At the table, he sipped his tea, black and bitter, until he heard the inevitable shuffling.

Before the accident, the earl had been an imposing man. Years of playing rugby had made him broad, as hard and firm as his temperament. But in the tumble from the carriage his leg had twisted, and he had never regained his fitness. Grey and sallow from too little sun, he refused to use a wheeled chair, or even a cane, so instead hobbled from his rooms to his study, reliant on the staff to keep him steady. He insisted on the strict observance of mealtimes and the old rituals, even though it was only the two of them and they mostly sat together in sullen silence.

Irving helped the earl into his chair. Most days, he drank tea before shaking out the paper to pass comment on the state of the world, but today he made straight for the paper.

'Let's hope I don't find my son in the headlines.' His mumble was half lost in the rustle of the pages. 'With any luck he has resisted the impulse to paw at well-dressed strumpets.'

Each day they played this game of snide comments and retorts, never openly talking about what had happened, letting it fester. Normally Hamish parried a reply, relishing the combat that fed his anger, but today, the thought of a snide sparring match brought no joy. Ignoring the bait, he reached into his pocket and pulled out the post card.

'What do you find so objectionable about the Abberton's?' he asked as he ran his fingers around the edges. 'Albert Abberton wasn't the only businessman in the street. And his wealth far exceeds ours. Even with his removal from the board, he remains a substantial shareholder. And that's before Iris sees a return on her business.'

His father grunted. 'Upstart trader. Thought he was better than he was. And adopting that bastard, elevating her higher than he should. He gave her pretentions.'

'Iris isn't a bastard. Her blood father was lost at sea, leaving her mother to model to make a living. And they are hardly pretentious, or upstarts. What is it then?'

His father grumbled, flicked out his paper and took up his tea.

All along, Iris had loved him, yet when he told her of his plans to find a wife, she hadn't flinched. And when he'd proposed, and she'd rebutted him, it was with a startling prescience about how his father might react, even though Hamish had never breathed a word of the earl's ire to her. Like she already knew.

Hamish allowed the pieces of memory to float. His mother's talk of Iris's success in entering society. His father's discussions with his old cronies about the wealth she would bring into a union. Lewis describing how attractive she had become. And suddenly, the fragments pulled together.

'She turned him down.'

The flash of shock across his father's face spoke more than any slander could. They had weighed Iris and deemed her acceptable as a bride for Lewis. And she had turned him down.

'But Lewis didn't care for her. He would have been miserable.'

'He knew what it meant to the family.' His father's voice began as a rumble, but soon amplified with anger. 'He would have done his duty, unlike you!'

'Just say it, you wish it had been me!' Hamish spat, years of anger and regret swelling, the loss of Iris chaffing, and the recurring pain of his father's disappointment, no matter how hard he worked or what he sacrificed, biting. 'You would gladly swap us.'

'Of course, I would!' The earl slammed his letters onto the table, upsetting the cutlery which clanged metallic against the plate. 'He had been at my side since he could stand. I taught him everything, and *he* understood. Not just the tenants and the books and the estate, but laws and legislature, all of it. And one loose wheel and you just filled his place!'

'I didn't bloody want to!' Hamish screeched back, sending his own setting rattling across the table. 'I lost my mother and my brother. You lost—'

Bitter words filled his mouth, and his tongue itched to shout *your wife who hated you and your lackey*, but something akin to fear, and a profound sadness, dashed across his father's face. Hamish saw then that his words could strike a terrible blow and shred what remained of the old man's heart.

He remembered his mother's beautiful smile. He remembered Lewis, not yet tall enough to see over the desk, being lifted onto their father's knee. Their private jokes, and the evenings they sat smoking together in the study as they discussed politics. Their easy comfort with one another.

'You lost more than a son. You lost your best friend. I only just realised. Father, I'm so sorry.'

The earl slumped back as if wounded. Perhaps he would have preferred the onslaught Hamish had been on the precipice of delivering, but hate had weighed far too heavy for too long, and now it fatigued him.

'I can't be Lewis,' he said, forcing his voice steady. 'And while my best is likely not good enough for you, I mean to do my best. I will see to the tenants, I will read your boring papers, I will open those books you've had Irving stack on my desk and take notes, anything.'

His father's eyes didn't soften, but only became more cautious, flicking like one of the new dogs after an unsuccessful hunt, unsure whether to whimper or snarl.

'But—' Hamish took up the *carte postale* and let his love for Iris fortify him. 'While I will be polite to any guests you choose to host at your table, I will not seek more than conversation. I will attend London for parliament, but I will not partake in the meat mart they call the season.'

'Your duty to your position includes providing an heir,' the earl growled.

'No, it does not. And if I never father an heir, the world will not end, because the entire bloody system is created to ensure there is *always* an heir. As you said, I did nothing and just became one! And if I cannot share my life with the woman I love, *my* best friend, a woman you deemed good enough for Lewis but would deny me out of spite, then I will not marry at all.'

His father's face turned cerise then took on a purple hue, like roast beetroot that had sat on the plate too long and begun to cool. 'You want your cousin, that indolent, practically illiterate lay about to be the next earl?'

'I am sure I won't care, Father. I'll be dead.'

His father's chin twitched, like he was chewing on his reply, before he threw his serviette onto the table. 'Fine. If that's the only way to keep this place from that imbecile, then marry the wench. Send a note, bring her here. The vicar can conduct the ceremony once the banns have been read.'

'It's not that simple.' While the prospect of his future filled him with trepidation, Hamish also found, for the first time, a glimmer of the righteousness he had craved, and obscurely enough, he had found it in Iris. 'A summons to the estate and a date with the vicar will not sway her. I must ask for her forgiveness, and then her hand. Properly. And then, I can only hope she says, "Yes". After all, I behaved terribly. I have been a rogue.'

His father rolled his eyes and murmured something which may have been *most ridiculous rogue imaginable,* but Hamish couldn't quite hear. The earl drummed his fingers against the table, then looked towards the door. 'Irving?'

'My Lord?' The valet stepped forward.

'My son has urgent business in London. Pack his things.'

As Irving gave a short bow, Hamish was sure the valet threw a wink his way before he strode from the room.

'Are you waiting for an invitation?' the earl snapped.

Hamish, who had frozen with shock, startled as if electrified. He grabbed a roll from the basket and tore into the crusty loaf, famished, then leapt from his seat, and with a short nod to his father from the door, raced after Irving, catching him on the stairs.

'First, we will need to stop by the vicarage,' he said between a mouthful of bread. 'I'll need some supplies, and a few reliable hands.'

CHAPTER
TWENTY-ONE

Steam swirled as it parted around Iris and Gena. Mason, up ahead, had piled their bags on a trolley and now stood at the entrance of King's Cross station, flailing for a cab.

'I don't know about these steam engines, miss,' Gena said. 'The modern era is much too fast for me. Next time, I would prefer a carriage.'

'A carriage from Dover? We'd be barely at Maidstone. As it is, we've made excellent time, especially after chancing the earlier steam ship from Calais.'

Gena clutched her stomach. 'Don't remind me, I'm still unsteady. Should we stop for tea? Perhaps that will help me settle.'

'For the past two weeks you've been grumbling about being abroad so long, and now we're here, you want to drag your feet? We can have tea at home. Now, where is Mason?'

Iris scanned the crowds for the tall, lean form of Mason, his black bowler lost in a sea of identical headwear. While not as homesick as Gena, she did crave a hot bath and her favourite teacup.

'There he is!' Up ahead, Mason heaved a trunk onto the back of a Hansom cab and the driver tied it down. 'Come on, Gena. A cup of tea awaits. You'll be right as rain in no time.'

As the cab lumbered through the streets, Iris burrowed her fingers tighter inside her muff, the soft rabbit pelt warming her fingertips. Now home and racing through the chill streets, the time away seemed to sit heavy. While she was abroad, Jonah had taken Papa on a short excursion to Brighton, his childhood home, in the hope that the familiar sights and smells would rouse his memory, and she was desperate to see them again. Jonah had made no hint in his letters if Papa had declined further, or was anything other than happy and well, but she knew that her uncertainty would not fade until she held his hand and kissed his brow herself.

Despite the cold of late autumn, the day was a rare, brilliant blue, the sort that could trick one into suspecting London was a pleasant place to live, and even wiped away the memory of dreary days for those who knew better. Tomorrow, she would need to write a report for the board of Spencer and Co, so they could discuss proposed travel routes and the types of excursions that might appeal to their clientele. Tomorrow, though. Today, she was simply a girl returning home.

The hansom cab turned onto Regent Street, past the house with the red side door to the gambling den Hamish had taken her, possibly his only vaguely successful attempt at being a rake. Now, having left the mutterings of scandal behind for a few months, the recollection of that night, and the one that followed, seemed, like London, beautiful and wondrous. It glowed inside her, a memory that would never be tainted no matter what gossip might follow her, or the cut of a turned back. The anger she felt had faded as she stood on the top of the Arc, looking along the tree-lined streets of Paris, and could only imagine the frustration Hamish had felt all those years as his dreams sat mouldering, and never receiving a word of thanks or care. She had sent him a *carte postale* as soon as she returned to street level, hoping that if nothing else, he would be inspired to find his own way into the wider world.

'It's a lovely day. Maybe you'd fancy a turn around the park before we get home? See the leaves changing?' Gena said. Her mittened hands clasped tight over each other, fidgeting in a way that Iris had thought was from the cold, but now, seemed more like worry.

'What has gotten into you?' Iris asked. 'You've been a bundle of nerves since we met Mason at the station. We are almost home. There, up ahead, is the sign to Honeysuckle Street.'

The brass rimmed plaque gleamed in welcome, the clop of the horse's hooves echoing dull as they moved onto the narrower street. The cab pulled up in front of Number 4. Mason leapt down and fumbled with the door. Iris took his hand and stepped out of the cab.

'I shall see to the bags and the driver, miss. You must be after that cup of tea.'

'Unless you are seeing to the driver with your own wages, I think I shall. And what on earth is going on at Number 6? Is someone building?'

Iris dug into her purse, retrieved a coin, and passed it to the driver. Mason hadn't replied, nor had he moved to unpack the trunks, but merely stood statuesque. 'Err... tea?' he asked, his eyes panicked.

Iris moved away from the cab and took a few steps towards Number 6, where Elise stood almost central, facing the vacant block. A basket of paper flowers rested on one hip as she gestured upwards, calling out to someone Iris did not recognise.

'Elise?'

Elise turned and nearly dropped the basket. 'Iris? Oh Iris, it's so good to see you. What are you doing here? You aren't due home until tomorrow.'

'We made good time and caught the earlier steamship. What is going on?'

Her friend seemed to have gone as mute as Mason. Iris took a step closer, her eyes scanning the site. They were building something, although at first, she thought it might be the construction of a new house, but it was clearly much smaller than any other house on Honeysuckle Street. Less than six feet wide and rising no more than eight, the squat frame of trimmed wooden boughs with a gabled roof was too small to be a worker's cottage. It had no floor, or walls, and seemed to be hammered together with wooden dowels and joins and lashed in the corners with rope.

'Elise? What is this?'

'Pass me the mallet,' a familiar voice called.

Iris used her arm to shadow her eyes, disbelieving her ears. 'Lord Dalton? Elise, why is Lord Dalton here?'

A man with a beam balanced on his shoulder turned. Iris didn't know him either, but as her eyes darted from face to face, she found a stark mix of friends and strangers, neighbours, and, judging from their clothes and a hint of accent in their chatter, out of towners. 'My lord,' the man called, before turning to where Hamish sat balanced on one of the beams, a length of cord in his hand, coatless, his navy-blue waistcoat flecked with sawdust. 'I think you have your dates wrong.'

'What do you mean, Irving?' Hamish leaned forward and swung the rope in a smooth arc, over the beam, before tugging it tighter. 'I checked the calendar this morning.' He chuckled, still not looking up from his work. 'I check every damn day.'

He eased back, his feet crossed beneath him to keep hold, his thigh muscles tensing against his trousers and one hand resting on the gable to hold his balance. The sky behind him framed his neat hair, and a slight shadow over his cheek highlighted a dimple. He looked first to the man, Irving, and then flicked to her. As recognition flooded his features, the easiness of his smile evaporated, replaced by confusion, and then panic.

'What's the date?' Hamish called. 'It's the twelfth, isn't it? I thought it was—'

'It's the twelfth,' Iris called back. 'We got an earlier connection. Lord Dalton, what are you doing here? What is all this?'

'No, no, no.' He unhooked himself from his perch and swung himself down, landing sure footed between the tussocks of grass. 'I had it all planned.'

'What did you have planned?'

'Your homecoming. I wanted it to be perfect.'

'But why?' she asked.

'Because I had something to ask you, but I knew I couldn't just ask. I had to do it right. But I've muffed that too. I can't be a rogue, and I can't be a gentleman.' Hamish ran a hand through his hair and turned back towards the structure, then kicked at the ground. 'Bollocks.'

He ground the dirt with his toe and stuffed his hand into his pockets. The boy she loved so well, still slightly petulant, still impulsive, hadn't been shaken from him.

'You could try just being you?' she said, moving closer and lifting his chin so that she could look into his eyes. 'Or are we so grown up we can no longer imagine?'

The sly dimple he kept tucked away appeared at the edge of a grin. He gestured behind to the wooden structure. 'I was building a castle,' he said, slightly serious but with excitement sparkling in his eyes. 'Well, not much of a castle. Barely a folly. But I hoped it would remind you of the ones we built when we were children. And Miss Delaney was going to arrange a musician to play *Home Again* because I know it's your favourite.'

Frowning in thought, Hamish cast about the group. Mason, who had been standing a few feet from the road and still holding her hat box, dropped it and scampered to stand beneath the gable, his deep stage voice thrumming, '*Home again, home again!*' And by the time he stood in front of the little castle, he had been joined by Gena, Mr Babbage, and a few of the others. Their slightly off-key harmony stumbled over the first few lines, but eventually settled into a decent ensemble. Iris snuffled a giggle, blinking hard to clear her eyes.

Hamish, seemingly buoyed, took hold of her hand and led her into the centre of the vacant block.

'I was going to be standing here, waiting, in a new suit—not from Quigley—' Hamish tugged his waistcoat straight, smoothed his hair, and rolled down his shirt sleeves. 'And all this was going to be finished and decorated.' He gestured at the mostly finished frame, then took a few, swift steps to Elise, picked out a couple of the paper flowers from her basket, and held them like a bouquet. 'And I was going to welcome you home with a bunch of irises that his grace has been growing in his greenhouse for me.' Iris took the paper daisies. She tried to say, 'Thank you,' but her mouth had gone dry. 'And I was going to ask you something, well, two things. But I hadn't quite worked out what I was going to say. Just the gist of it.'

Iris's breath stilled and her heart thumped hard against her ribs. 'What were you going to say? Just the... just the gist of it.'

'I was going to say that I'm so sorry I hurt you. And while the injury I inflicted on you is unforgivable, I hoped you might still forgive me.'

Hamish tapped at his pocket, then mumbled a curse under his breath. A light film of sweat covered his brow. He looked to the flowers in her hand and picked out a white paper daisy. 'And even though I already asked, and you said no, as you should have, I was going to ask you again.' He twisted the stem so that it circled into a wide green band, and the flower sat flat, like a precious gem in its setting. 'I was going to drop to one knee.' As he said the words, he did just that. 'And I was going to say something like...' He chewed his lip in thought. 'Iris Diana Abberton. Tallier of numbers extraordinaire. Daughter of a goddess, and a goddess yourself. The wild girl of Honeysuckle Street. My oldest, dearest friend, the one I love above all others, and the one I always will. Would you deign to step from your pedestal and marry a mere, unworthy mortal such as myself?'

Hamish held out the paper flower, the petals slightly curled, his eyes hope and agony.

'But your father. He would never accept me,' she said, her heart aching at the memory of his father's tirade against her.

'The old coot approves. In his way,' he added, with a smirk that made Iris think she'd rather not know what the old man's way was. 'I promise, this is just me. No thoughts of scandal, or revenge. Just me, asking if you will forgive me, and will you be my wife?'

Iris held her breath until it hurt, not in deliberation, but because she knew of all the breathtaking places she had seen, there would be no *carte postales* of this, and she wanted to remember it, always. The sun lighting his face. The way his fingers trembled. The shuffling silence of those around them. And, most of all, the exquisite feeling of love and belonging that twisted and bloomed through her.

'Yes,' she said, her voice hoarse.

'Yes, you forgive me? Or yes, you'll marry me?'

'Both, you dolt.'

Joy fractured the uncertainty in his eyes, and Hamish grabbed her hand, crammed the paper daisy onto her finger, before leaping to his feet and enclosing her in his arms. His lips, still warm from work, found hers, and even with the claps and cheers erupting around them, Iris melted into his embrace as if the world was composed of just them two.

When they broke apart, Hamish rested his forehead against hers. 'I love you, Lady La-di-dah. I always have. I was just too thick to know it.'

'I love you too. *Hamish.*' She relished the old familiarity of speaking his name without titles and the sound of releasing what she had kept bottled for far too long, and for the first time, her love felt light enough to skim the clouds. She stepped back and looked up at the gable. 'I feel terrible for ruining your surprise. It would have been beautiful.'

Hamish cocked his head, then gave a cheeky grin. 'Maybe it doesn't have to be wasted?'

Epilogue

The following day, Hamish and Iris celebrated their commitment to one another beneath the beautifully decorated wooden castle. Mason, wearing an old costume from his West End days, officiated as the priest. Mr Abberton gave away the bride, and as he kissed her cheek, he whispered, 'Keep an eye on the biscuits.'

Of course, it wasn't the formal, legally binding wedding ceremony—that would be held weeks later in the chapel near Caplin House, after the banns had been read, and with the old earl in grudging attendance. But with the London sun daring to shine two days in a row, surrounded by their friends, family, and new business associates, Hamish and Iris would always look back on this day as the one that began their journey as husband and wife.

Meanwhile, Spencer, perched in a low branch beside the Abberton house, gave a lazy tail flick, his body rumbling with delight as Hamish lifted the veil and kissed the bride. Not so much for the kissing, or the union of the two who had first fed him scraps while a kitten, but because from this perch, the smell of hot sausages and frying bacon wafted on the breeze, and he knew that if he squeezed through the lower window, he'd likely catch a few stray cuts in the kitchen, and if he made his way upstairs and nudged against the guests' legs during the wedding breakfast, a few of them would drop a morsel discreetly to the floor for him to nibble.

Standing, stretching, Spencer arched and began to ease his way down the broad trunk of the oak tree when he spotted something move across the vacant block and through a hole in the fence ... was that a tail? Black, tipped with white. He sniffed the breeze, his whiskers twitching in anticipation of a fight to defend his territory ... but this new arrival wasn't a tom.

Spencer leapt lightly to the ground and trotted the breadth of the vacant block, before slinking through the narrow gap in the fence.

Crumbs would keep. He had a duty, after all, to welcome all new arrivals to the street.

THE END

Historical note

Honeysuckle Street is not a real London street. It is a total invention, because to find a street that is historically accurate that allowed my characters to play out the drama of their lives would take an inordinate amount of research and deep knowledge of town planning and post-war reconstruction that it would consume my life almost completely. So, rather than delve into a never ending pit of research frustration, I decided to create a fairly typical London street in the late Victorian era, and from there, write my stories.

In chapter nine, Hamish arrives on the Abberton doorstep singing *I've Been Roaming,* George Sloane, 1825.

In chapter twenty-one, Mason and friends sing *Home Again, Home Again, From a Foreign Shore,* M.S.Pike, no date.

Alzheimer's was not described as a medical condition in scientific literature until 1906, although it was recognised and discussed in medical communities in the 18th century. Families who experienced having a loved one slip from them faced an incredibly traumatic and perplexing situation, one they didn't understand any more than the doctors offering advice. The trauma, confusion and grief is still felt today, for having a name does not decrease the heartbreak of watching proud family member slip away. The experience of Iris and her father is not meant to be all encompassing or historically representative, it is simply a reflection of my own lived experience of losing a beloved family member to this horrible disease. I have always processed emotion and grief through my writing, and Brucey, I guess you got me here. We miss you. xxx

A Song and a Snowflake

Before Iris and Hamish scandalised Honeysuckle Street, there was Charlise and Sinclair...

A woman seeking redemption at the end of a church aisle...

Beautiful songbird Charlise Hartright is ruined.

Introverted, shy and grieving her mother's loss, she would do anything to restore the family name, even commit to a loveless match, if it means her beloved sister Elise will have a chance at finding her own happiness.

A man out to make his own name...

Sinclair McIntyre has travelled halfway across the world to pursue of his own destiny. Tired of being in the shadow of his older brothers, he is determined to do things his own way to become an independent, self-made man.

A future laid out before each of them...

But with a song

And a snowflake

Everything will change.

Sign up to my newsletter An Old Fashioned Quickie to receive your FREE copy of A Song and a Snowflake.

aliviafleur.com

Acknowledgements

The idea for a book series set within a fictional street came to me while I was under observation in the emergency department. The writing of the book happened while I was in recovery. Too sick to work, not sick enough to sleep, pouring out words for an idea that felt bigger than the short stories I had already published gave me something to focus on during those days that even now I look back on and can only see as a blur. So first I would like to thank everyone who works in the health profession. For the sore feet, the tired smiles, and long hours. Thank you.

Thank you to my cover designer, the amazing Evelyne Labelle at Carpe Librum Book Design.

Special thanks to my editor, Adrianne Jenks from Adrianne Jenks Editorial, who has put up with all my phaffing and rewrites with patience. We got there!

To my amazing writer friends, Samantha L. Valentine and Eve Moxey, for reading my crummy drafts and helping me sort them out. To Sam especially for being the most encouraging person, and for believing in my stories when I've had enough of them. And to Eve for answering all my ridiculous questions on corsets, bustles and chemises. And the memes!

And to the fabulous Mr Fleur. My love, my one, my only. Thank you for everything, everyday.

About

Alivia Fleur writes steamy romantic fiction for history lovers. In her stories, curious and consenting adults explore their desires as they search for their own happy ever after.

Alivia lives with her husband on a farm a long way from anywhere interesting. When not herding sheep or checking fences, she enjoys reading romance, drinking tea and eating cake, preferably all at once.

Upcoming releases and newsletter signup can be found at AliviaFleur.com

Made in the USA
Coppell, TX
08 February 2025

45609559R00132